Olive Thorne Miller

Our Home Pets

how to keep them well and happy

Olive Thorne Miller

Our Home Pets
how to keep them well and happy

ISBN/EAN: 9783337405755

Printed in Europe, USA, Canada, Australia, Japan

Cover: Foto ©Andreas Hilbeck / pixelio.de

More available books at **www.hansebooks.com**

Our Home Pets

How to Keep Them Well and Happy

BY

OLIVE THORNE MILLER,

Illustrated

NEW YORK

HARPER & BROTHERS PUBLISHERS

1894

CONTENTS

CONTENTS

ILLUSTRATIONS

—

OUR HOME PETS

I

IS IT CRUEL TO KEEP BIRDS?

"Bird of the amber beak,
Bird of the golden wing,
Thy dower is thy carolling;
Thou hast not far to seek
Thy bread, nor needest wine
To make thine utterance divine;
Thou art canopied and clothed,
And unto song betrothed."
—STEDMAN.

A GOOD deal of sentiment is expended upon caged birds. From tender hearts, and from others not so tender, we often hear, " I can't bear to keep a bird in a cage!" Now, without in any way advocating the caging of birds, I must say that there are two sides to this, as to most questions.

It is true the captive is at the mercy of his

owner; his food depends upon some one's memory; his comfort, his very life, are in the power of another; but the same is true of the household dog and cat, still more of the horse. Moreover, the last-named animal is so much worse off that he is made to work, and often sadly abused by his owner, yet we hear little sympathy expressed for his state of slavery.

It is cruel to capture an adult bird, accustomed to freedom and to caring for himself, and confine him in a cage; it is worse than cruel, it is brutal, to neglect to provide carefully for his comfort when thus imprisoned. But that a captive bird, *properly caught* and *properly cherished*, must necessarily be unhappy I emphatically deny, and my opinion is based upon several years' close study of birds in confinement.

By " properly caught," I mean taken from the nest, or when just out of it. By " properly cherished," I mean not only fed and watered as regularly and carefully as we attend to our own physical needs, but in every other way made as happy as is possible by loving attention and thoughtful consideration.

As to the canary, born in a cage, of caged

ancestry, he is utterly incapacitated for freedom. So far from being a kindness to give him his liberty, it is a positive cruelty. He has never sought food or shelter, he has no notion of doing either, and he must inevitably perish. Birds that have been taken from the nest are in a similar condition of ignorance. Unless kept in captivity a very short time, and afterwards supplied with food till they learn to care for themselves, to thrust them out is like taking a child brought up in luxury and forcing him into the streets to pick up his own living. This comparison is not in the least exaggerated. A young bird is taught by his parents where and how to get his food. Close observers may see this instruction going on all summer, when nesting is over and young birds are out. If, then, this period of instruction is passed in a house, and he is adult when turned adrift, there is no one to teach him, and he must learn by hard experience, or die in the attempt.

I have read stories of children being induced to set free their pets, because they would be so much happier. One in particular I remember, because I was so indignant about it, where the bird refused to be left in the park, but flew back several times and alighted on its owners, and they actually had to scheme to get away from it. It was told as a self-sacrificing and virtuous deed, when, as a matter of fact, it was undoubtedly pure cruelty, and that bird, accustomed to care and shelter, probably died of want and exposure.

Another use of a caged bird, or any captive, that is of great value as I look at it, is the opportunity it gives for lessons in consideration and care for others, and love and kindness to animals. It has been ascertained by statistics, carefully gathered from training-schools and prisons, that very few men who in boyhood owned or cared for a pet animal, or who were instructed in kindness to the lower orders, are to be found among criminals. This fact, which should not astonish us when we think of the elevating tendency of unselfishness, puts into the hands of parents and teachers a powerful weapon for good. Not only does the pet bird or beast entertain and amuse the boy, but, under proper direction, it trains him in gentle ways, in a sense of justice, and it goes far to insure an honest life.

There is a further point to be considered. Birds *are* caged, and have been since the beginning of the world — so far as we know; no one of us can help it. To rescue one or more from the miserable conditions of a bird store, and make them happy in our homes, is a deed of charity, not an unkindness. If we could arouse all over the world a sentiment that would prevent the catching of birds at all, I should rejoice with all my heart. But since we know that is impossible, let us try to comfort ourselves by redeeming from uncomfortableness every one that we can.

An English lady whom I know has a delightful way of taming the birds on her place without making them prisoners. It is thus: When they are about ready to leave the nest, she removes a bird — perhaps two — from the parents' care, assuming the duties of the parent herself, and feeding her captives carefully every half-hour from four in the morning till dark. At the same time she talks to them, and gets them familiar with her. When they are full-grown, and not at all afraid of her, she opens her windows and lets them out, keeping the food and water supply in plain sight, within the always open casement. Her reward is a charming colony of birds in her grounds, who come freely into her house, accept food from her hands, sing for her, bring their wild mates and their little ones, and in every way are enchanting daily visitors. But she is careful not to retain them too long, and to keep a supply of food convenient for them. Birds so educated have been known to stay out-of-doors all summer, and take up winter-quarters in the house year after year.

But even when the birds caught are grown up, if the second condition is carried out and they are "properly cherished," they frequently become so attached to their homes that they will not accept liberty when it is offered. Nor need we be surprised at this. The life of a bird in freedom is by no means so easy as it appears; an intelligent observer soon comes to know that he is at work nearly every hour of the day, beginning several hours before we are out of bed. When there are young ones to be fed, the parents are absolutely driven from morning till night, and, as their lovers well know, nearly all bird music ceases during those hard-worked days.

Now when one of these little workers is made comfortable and happy in a house, and well fed, without exertion of his own, he becomes—exactly as does a human being—disinclined to work. Thrusting him out of his easy home is, in fact, condemning him to a life of hard labor, which is often as distasteful to him as the loss of an income is to a man. To be sure, a captive is deprived of fresh air and his natural out-of-door life, but when he is used to these conditions it is with him a matter of choice—as it is with many of us—between a life of bondage without labor, and freedom with it.

I have had birds, more than one, who did not care even to leave their cages, who would stay inside all day with the door wide open, perfectly cheerful and contented. But it must be remembered that I spared no thought or labor to supply my birds with everything that would add to their comfort or their pleasure.

I do not deny that most caged birds are unhappy; and because I love them, I am generally made miserable by every one I see, panting and pleading for relief with eager

eyes, in the glare of the hot sun, or against a
burning brick wall; shivering in the draught
of an open window; shrinking from the falling rain and the unaccustomed night air;
smothered in muslin up to their roof, or
starving on a thimbleful of seed and about
as much water.　But this is not because they
are caged; it is because of the thoughtlessness or carelessness of their keepers.

I regard it as just as bad to keep a bird without giving due care and attention to its needs
as to leave a horse in a stable without food
or exercise, or a dog chained to a post day
after day and week after week.　Looked at
in' one way, indeed, it is worse, for a dog
can make himself very disagreeable, and re-
mind people of his presence, while the horse,
representing a considerable sum of money,
is usually thought of; but the poor bird, not
worth much in dollars, with a language un-
noticed and unintelligible to most of us, can
only die, as thousands of them do die every
year, victims to the neglect of somebody.
This is truly an outrage, and no sympathy
that is expended on these unfortunate creatures is wasted.

One thing more I should like to say. Although I maintain that a captive can be made entirely contented, I never have, and I never intend to have, a bird caught or caged for my pleasure or my study. And again I say, most emphatically, that unless a person is able and willing to give daily thought and care to a bird, it is bitterly cruel, even wicked, to assume the charge of one.

My position on the caged-bird question thus fully defined, I wish to give some suggestions in regard to making birds not only comfortable, but happy.

II

WHICH SHALL WE CHOOSE?

HAVING decided to keep a bird, the important question is, naturally, what shall be chosen out of the great variety of native and foreign birds to be found in our bird stores?

It may help to a decision to inquire a little into your motives. Why do you want a bird? Is it to put a finishing touch to a room, to entertain you with song, to amuse the children, or to be a companion to you?

If the decoration of a room is the object, your way is plain; get a brilliant-hued parrot, or a

> " Cockatoo, creamy and white,
>   With roses under his feathers
> That flash across the light,"

put it into a gorgeous gilded cage, upon a handsome standard, in the middle of a bay-window, and the thing is done. If you want a singer, choose a canary or a mocking-bird; either one,

THE BROWN THRUSH

properly encouraged, will sing enough to satisfy the most exacting; in fact, most owners of these birds are forced to keep a cloth cover for the cage, to moderate their too exuberant song, or to relegate the irrepressible to solitary confinement in some retired apartment, so that people may talk, and rest their weary ears. So be sure of your object.

If what you desire is something to amuse the children, by all means procure a big cage, and fill it with a dozen or two of the pretty little African finches, who live amicably together, and with their endless pranks furnish never-failing entertainment to the little folk.

If you care for a delightful companion, I recommend to you our own native birds, the most intelligent you can get; perhaps one of the thrush family—the wood-thrush, robin, or thrasher, or a bluebird, or, better still, a pair.

If your heart longs for the king of singers, and one of the most intelligent birds in the whole list, I suggest the clarin, a Mexican bird.

> "He is the poet bird, who sings
> Through joy, through sorrow, through all things;"

but I warn you that you must love him, and let him know it, or he will be little more than a shadow in your house. He is so sensitive in organization that you must win his heart before you can enjoy his finest song, at least in our climate, so far from his home.

The choice may depend somewhat upon another thing; birds are divided into seed-eaters and soft-billed. The former class, which includes parrots, canaries, and all finches, is easily cared for, the food being ready for use when bought. The latter class — thrushes, bluebirds, and all insect eaters — must have soft food like mocking-bird food, ants' eggs, meat, etc., all of which require preparation and greater care.

To speak in detail of the more common varieties to be procured in our stores. The qualities of the canary it is not necessary to mention; he is so common that every one is familiar with them. I will begin, therefore, with the next best known, the parrot. Of this bird there are almost innumerable varieties, of nearly every color and size. The gray African, a solemn-looking personage in light dove-color with a brilliant red tail, is considered the most intelligent in the matter of talking, though most of the family may be taught that accomplishment. Cockatoos do not learn so readily to speak, but they can squawk and scream with the loudest. Their almost incurable passion for making unpleasant noises, especially loud shrieks, is a serious objection to these birds, and one should consider the state of her own nerves before consenting to harbor one. All the tribe — paroquets, cockatoos, macaws, and even the sentimental love-birds —are noisy and often unbearable in a room. On the other hand, they are affectionate, ingenious in mischief, and exceedingly entertaining pets, besides being easily kept happy and in health, and very long lived. I never knew of a person making a companion of one of the family without becoming warmly attached to it.

The mocking-bird, so often kept in captivity for his song, is really a most interesting inmate of our homes for other qualities—his spirited manners, his intelligence, and his fertile wit. No bird of my acquaintance will think of so many droll things to do, and be so certain to do them, as this one. He is not so affectionate as some others, but when he does become attached to people he is well able to show his preference. If allowed his freedom in a room, he will be so busy and happy, with occupations he can invent for himself, that he will not be troublesome with excessive singing.

In considering the less-known cage birds, let us begin with the one most frequently seen, the American robin. This bird is easily tamed, being intelligent and naturally fearless. He soon learns that no harm is intended to him, and that behind his wires he need not dread the human being who, out-of-doors, he never thought of fearing. He takes kindly to life in our houses, and especially to the food that he finds on our tables. He is also affectionate, readily becoming fond of individuals. When free in a house he is particularly entertaining, ready in invention, and doing things no one would expect of him. He is observing, having his own opinion of everything he sees, and well able to make his wishes understood. As a singer he is not noted in captivity, although if kept away from other birds, and not allowed too much liberty, he will sing.

The thrasher, or, more properly, brown thrush, considerably resembles the robin in confinement, though he has none of the thrush composure, being very restless in manner. He is always busy, always interested, and full of devices to amuse himself and you. Sometimes, especially if kept apart from other birds, he will sing beautifully in a cage, but I must confess there was always too much society, and too much going on, for any thrasher to sing in my house.

The thrushes—wood, hermit, and Wilson's—are all lovely and winning birds in a house; but it is difficult to make them at home, or to reconcile them to captivity. They are reserved, and rarely familiar with other birds. They do not go into wild panics, or make mad efforts to escape; but they look straight at one out of beautiful, untamable eyes, in a way that makes it very hard for a bird-lover to keep them confined a moment. They do not condescend to pranks, and amusement is the last thing we must expect from this dignified family.

A rollicking, mischief-loving relative of the thrushes is the cat-bird, and for eccentric freaks and lively frolics, I do not know his equal. The mocking-bird is nearest like him in these respects. I will engage that no house that possesses a cat-bird at liberty will ever lack entertainment or suffer from ennui.

The Baltimore oriole is an exceedingly decorative bird. He is susceptible to kindness, and if taken young and kept alone, becomes very tame and friendly. He does not sing except in the spring, nor does he show so much intelligence as the thrush family. He is, however, inquisitive, and he delights to pick things to pieces, especially lace, and fabrics in which the threads are distinct. He will pry into unaccustomed places, behind and under furniture, creep through blinds or gratings, and pick holes in the wall-paper. He is interesting, and one readily becomes attached to him.

Bluebirds are charming in a house, gentle, always uttering their sweet little warble, and bringing to mind the orchards and

> "the long sweet hours
> That follow the fragrant feet of June."

They are affectionate and easily tamed, and half a dozen will live amicably together. Never

THE CATBIRD

mischievous in pranks, they are delightful to look at and listen to, but not so amusing, nor apparently so intelligent, as those already spoken of.

The Virginia cardinal is a favorite cage bird, both on account of his beauty and his song. Indeed, an English lady who had one of these birds for years declares that he is a finer singer than the nightingale. That is a high compliment for our bird, for the nightingale is famed in song and story, and by many considered the finest singer in the world. The cardinal is not specially interesting as a pet. His song and his brilliant coat are the sum of his attractions. If his food dish is well supplied, and his comfort in other respects attended to, he becomes entirely reconciled to captivity, but never—at least in the room with other birds—familiar with his human neighbors. I have heard of cardinals kept alone who became friendly and affectionate, but I have myself owned several of them, and never felt acquainted with one. To my taste, the female is much more lovely, and a sweeter singer than her mate, having softer tints and not so loud a voice.

The rose-breasted grosbeak, nearly related to the cardinal, is, in my opinion, a more beautiful bird, though not so well known. He is black and white, with an exquisite rose-colored shield on his breast. He resembles his more brilliant cousin in characteristics, though he is not so fine nor so persistent a singer. He is, indeed, rather shy, and not particularly satisfactory as a pet.

The orchard oriole, while not so brilliant in coloring as the Baltimore, is a ready and fine singer, and a beautiful bird. The female is a charming songster and a pretty bird, in soft yellow olive, with bright blue legs and feet. The male of this family I have not found pleasant in disposition. He is quarrelsome and jealous, and would do better alone than in the room with others. One that I kept fretted his mate to death.

The red-winged blackbird is a pleasing house bird, with a bewitching wild song of few notes, which, however, breathes the very spirit of the woods, and is most attractive to wood-lovers. He is a seed-eater, and requires little care, but does not show so great intelligence as the thrushes.

A beautiful bird, but very difficult to keep in health, is the scarlet tanager. He does not, in a house, readily accept any food but living flies, and he never ceases to regret his liberty. If he has the companionship of several of his kind, he is more likely to be contented; but he does not care for other birds, and he is almost sure to mope and die. I know of but one bird-dealer in New York who succeeds in keeping this bird alive, and I think his secret is in giving him plenty of company of his own family.

The golden-wing woodpecker, or flicker, though extremely wild at first, and hard to accustom to mocking-bird food, if carefully treated, without being frightened, will become tame and friendly. His song is very low and rarely uttered, but his calls and cries are pleasant, and suggestive of woods and summer days. I do not regard him as a desirable pet, and much thought is needful to make him happy, such as supplying the cage with fresh branches on which to hammer.

The blue-jay is a more than usually fascinating pet when taken from the nest and never accustomed to wild life. He reminds one of a mischievous child, and he is one of the busiest and happiest of captives, though he must be watched closely, or he will destroy books and furniture without end. As a cage bird he is not specially interesting. It is only when free in a room or house that his capabilities have play.

The bobolink is of a peculiar organization, madly afraid of every human being—and no wonder! utterly declining to believe in one's good intentions, and beating himself to death against the wires. I have found him too painful to look at, and impossible to keep in captivity for a week. When a bobolink's confidence *is* won, and he is away from other birds, I have heard of his being a delightful and companionable pet, though I never had the pleasure of seeing one. I can hardly conceive of this bird as singing in confinement, but I have authentic accounts from a bobolink-lover of at least three who have kept their respective human homes in charming music all the season through. To secure this, weeks and months of care and pains would not be lost, for his song is one of the enchantments of a New England June.

Birds too large to be conveniently kept in a city often make agreeable pets for the country, where room is not so limited. The crow is one of the most attractive, being a very wide-awake personage, with plenty of ideas, and wit enough to carry them out. He becomes much attached to the human race, as soon as he is convinced they do not want to eat him. He must be watched, however, for his great propensity is to carry off and secrete silver, or anything that strikes his fancy. As to deserting his home, and going away with his wild relatives, if properly treated and made comfortable he will rarely do so.

Owls of several kinds afford no end of diversion when tamed; but they, too, need the run of larger quarters than a house.

The magpie is full of fun and frolic, and learns to talk, but one needs a private detective to keep him out of mischief.

Of the foreign birds are many with which we are familiar in cages. The English goldfinch, a pleasant little fellow, readily accustoming himself to a cage, and a sweet singer without much variety; the song-thrush, a charming bird and a sweet singer, as is also the English blackbird, the latter with capacity for eccentricity rarely equalled in any of the feathered folk. The skylark, a favorite cage bird in his native land, does not flourish well with us, according to my experience. He is exceedingly shy, and is some extra trouble, as he needs, every few days, a fresh bit of turf to keep him happy.

The starling, in his quaint speckled dress, is a social and friendly fellow, droll in his ways, with the queerest song of any bird I know.

The Brazilian cardinal is a beautiful bird in soft dove-color with brilliant scarlet head. He is a tireless and rather loud singer, but bright and merry, and easily kept in health and spirits.

This list is surely long enough for every one to select from, and every bird mentioned has been for sale in New York bird stores, though, perhaps, not all at one time.

III

TO GET HIM HOME

ON starting out in search of an American bird—if you decide to have one—the first experience will be discouraging. Every dealer will deny that he has an American bird, in spite of the mocking-birds, South American parrots, and cardinal-grosbeaks which are almost always to be found in his stock. The truth is, that he so little regards the birds asked for that he really does not remember them. If you will walk slowly down the store and look for yourself into all the cages, you will be almost sure to see a robin or a bluebird tucked into some obscure corner as not worthy of notice.

Remembering this curious idiosyncrasy of the dealers, which I have often noticed, you must make up your mind to search for yourself, and having found a bird, make arrangements to have him taken home. The best way, and one that I strongly urge, is to take him yourself. If you do not attend to the matter, the bird-dealer, who regards the little creatures in his cages as so much merchandise, may put the frightened bird into a common pasteboard box, with no perch, where the unfortunate prisoner slides and scrambles around in the dark, during his whole trip to your house, arriving wild and tired out, and more than ever convinced of the cruelty of man. I have known one to be so terrorized by this experience that he never recovered from it, but was a shy, nervous fellow forever after.

Or, if not into a paper box, he may be thrust into one of the small German wooden cages in which canaries travel from Europe. These cages are simply idiotic for any bird bigger than a canary, for the reason that they have two perches, one about an inch and a half from each end. A bird too long to perch so near the bars can only rest on the floor between, with tail and wings held in unnatural positions. It is almost impossible for one to be carried in this way without being frightened by the cramped quarters. Usually the

BALTIMORE ORIOLES IN FREEDOM

plumage is materially injured, and often a wing is broken, or tail feathers pulled out by his struggles.

The way I have adopted is vastly better than these. I have two conveyances, one or other of which I take when I go bird-hunting. One is a small-sized, square-cornered splint basket, perhaps eight by ten inches in size, with a cover and handle. To prepare it for use, I cover the bottom with several thicknesses of paper, which are easily renewed, then fasten a good-sized perch across the middle, an inch or two above the floor, holding it firmly by a tack through from the outside. Into one corner I fasten with fine wire a small deep cup for water, into the opposite corner a cup for food. The basket, being woven, lets in plenty of light and air. A bird as large as a robin has enough room, and, as I carry it carefully, he is not afraid to eat and drink if he wishes.

The other carriage, which I use for smaller birds, is one of the wooden cages above mentioned, made over, first by a thorough scrubbing and scalding, and secondly by removing the absurd perches at the ends, and placing one across the middle, so that head and tail are both accommodated in natural attitudes. This done, I wrap the cage in buff or white wrapping-paper, making a nice package that I am willing to carry, and tying it up in such a way that one end has no string across it. Then I take scissors and cut the paper on the left-open end, across the top, and down the corners on each side, leaving it whole at the bottom. This makes a paper door opening over the wooden door.

The reason for all this care is that a bird may not be scared to death by the rattle of paper in doing up his cage, and it is necessary to cover him, to screen him from seeing things and people about him, which will drive him wild. When my door is complete, I arrange a string in such a way that I can tie it up or open it without disturbing the fastenings of the rest of the string.

When my bird is chosen, I untie this special string, fold back the paper door, and draw up the round wooden bars that form the door of the cage. Then the bird, already caught by the dealer, is gently loosened at the door, and instantly fastened in by slipping the wooden bars back to place; the paper door is quietly closed, the string tied, and he is not at all startled. A bird arriving at home in either of these conveyances is calm and unhurt, and he has no terror of me.

To change him into a cage which I have already prepared with food and water, and a cover laid over if he is wild, I first open the cage door, then place the door of the travelling cage against it, having turned back the paper door. Then I draw out the bars that keep him in the small cage, and he is sure to step at once into the large one.

To get one out of the basket above mentioned is a little more difficult operation. I hold the basket slightly opened before the door, with my hands or a cloth over the ends, so that he can get out only one way. He is certain to hop out as soon as he sees a good opening with apparently no one watching him.

When he is safely housed and the door shut, I leave him alone. If not covered up, I walk away and pay no attention to him nor come near his cage. I sit down afar off, and read or write, or occupy myself in some way, till he gets used to his new apartment. He will look at everything with the most eager interest, the room, the other birds, if there are any, and his new cage. Almost any bird will appreciate the improvement in his quarters, and begin to try them by jumping from perch to perch. Then he will learn where his food is, and lastly begin to eat and drink. All this should be accomplished quietly, without excitement, and to do so he must be left alone, and especially not be stared at.

The next day he will begin to feel some confidence in you, and you may come quietly and slowly up to him, put in fresh food and water, and speak gently to him, but not look at him much when near. A few days of this careful treatment will do wonders towards reassuring the trembling captive, and preparing him for feeling acquainted, and from that to growing tame and becoming attached to you. It makes months of difference in taming a bird, the way he is brought home.

A very wild bird should always be covered with a light cloth so that he cannot see people. I once brought home a frantically wild golden-wing woodpecker, who beat himself against the bars as though he would kill himself. I swathed his big cage in a light woollen shawl, leaving about three inches uncovered at one end. Then, before he noticed the opening, I seated myself with my back to the cage and a hand-mirror in my hand, in which I could see him, while he did not think I was looking. Then I kept perfectly still.

In a few minutes a long beak was thrust from behind the shawl screen, and a large eye came slowly beyond the edge. There he paused, and looked at me, at the room, the ceiling, the window near him, and the bird opposite. I remained silent with my back towards him, and he studied his new world for several minutes, then retreated behind the shawl.

Each day I made the opening a little wider, and changed the dishes from behind the screen so that he saw only my hand, and in a week I had, inch by inch, taken off the cover and given him the full view of the room. This woodpecker, though I never make the least effort to tame a bird, became so familiar that he would hop on to me, and stand still and let me pick him up, which I never knew any other creature in feathers to do.

IV

TO TAME HIM

THERE are three, yes four, possible degrees in our relations with a bird. In the first, his fear is overcome; in the second, he is made happy; in the third, he is tamed; in the fourth, he is humanized.

The first step of his progress, which in the majority of cases he never gets beyond, is essential to his comfort and our own, and the sooner it is taken the better. I have already suggested in a previous chapter that the cage of a very wild bird, until he gets accustomed to our presence, should be covered. Not until he can endure to see people about him without going into a panic, can the first step be taken.

A good way to do this is to place the cage on the table or desk beside you, going on with your occupation as usual, and not often looking at him. That is, if your occupation is a quiet one, reading, writing, or hand sewing. I should never put a bird by a sewing-machine, nor near any machine making sudden or violent motions.

If the stranger sees he is not observed, he studies you and your surroundings well; he gets used to being near you, and at length loses his terror of you. Then you may begin to speak to him and take notice of him, and when that no longer frightens him, to offer him dainties. This must be done gradually; you can't force a bird to lose his fear, and you must remember that with him we have a race terror to overcome, something that his parents and his parents' parents have instilled into him. Impatience and attempts to hasten progress make things worse—that is, if you really wish to gain the bird's goodwill.

Birds can be made what is called tame by the heroic process often practised on parrots by the natives who catch them, and sometimes by the dealers. It is a curious performance, but so far from overcoming their fear, it intensifies it to a point of abject slavishness, painful to one who loves birds. It is thus: First protecting the hand by heavy leathern gloves, the tamer seizes the wild creature by the legs and drags it out of the cage. The parrot has no notion of submitting to fate, and it shrieks, struggles, and bites savagely, while the tamer holds it firmly with the left hand, and strokes its back with the right. It now becomes a question of strength of will and physical endurance, for the tamer continues his stroking till the bird gives up, whether it be hours or days (including part of the nights), as it is in the case of a bird of spirit.

The tamer must remain in a room alone with his pupil, and must never give up his efforts till he yields. The poor captive often holds out till nearly dead of hunger and fatigue, but when he is finally conquered, it is for good and all. Though he is tamed, however, he is not won. He always has the bearing of a slave who obeys from fear, and naturally, he is a pitiful sight to a bird-lover.

Having accustomed the bird to your presence, the next step is to establish friendly relations with him, and to make him happy, something that is almost universally over-

THE CARDINAL GROSBEAK

looked by keepers of birds. Begin to talk to him, sing or whistle to him, give him something he likes; in a word, make him feel acquainted. He will be as ready to respond to these attentions as a child or a dog, and it will make him as happy. How many birds and other pets live in our houses year after year and get hardly a word or look from us! They are ignored as if they were wooden images or music machines, instead of fellow-creatures with sentiments and emotions like our own. If you have never tried it, you will be surprised to see how quickly the little fellow will answer a kind word, how he will wriggle his small body, and show in every movement that he is pleased, that he reciprocates your good-will. Some birds—notably canaries—will answer with their sweet call every time you speak, and keep it up as long as you do.

Let me caution you never to allow a bird to be teased or annoyed. Many boys and men who should know better delight in amusing themselves in that way. It may look droll to see a bird in a rage, scolding, beating his wings, snapping at a finger, and in other ways

showing that his evil passions are aroused,
but it ruins him for agreeable house companionship. It develops bad temper and disagreeable ways, such as squawking in jays,
screaming in parrots, and harsh scolding in
others. It makes them irritable, malicious to
other birds, and often to children.

To make him thoroughly happy, a bird in a
house needs some amusement; he pines for
something to interest him, and, like a child
kept in, he should be provided with playthings. A pet paroquet that I knew once,
though he had the freedom of his master's
house, was furnished with a small basket of
playthings, a bunch of keys, a bit of chain, a
spool or two, a few marbles, and other things.
The bird knew as well as any child that the
basket and its contents were his, and he made
a great row if any one touched them. Many
times a day he got down his basket, and
amused himself an hour at a time with its
treasures.

Another bird — a parrot — had to be enter-
tained every day, and if people were busy and
he were neglected, he helped himself to playthings. A favorite object was a spool of

thread, from which he cut the contents with his sharp beak, and then demolished the spool. A lead-pencil or pen-handle to bite and reduce to slivers was acceptable; and, indeed, he could amuse himself with almost anything, and, when he was not supplied with a stock of his own, he was always in mischief.

A thrush I once had used to amuse himself with the hanging fringe of a towel laid over a chair. He would run at it, try to pull out the threads, and, holding by the beak, swing back and forth with great relish.

A crumpled newspaper laid on the floor is often a source of pleasure, also a ball that rolls easily, as a marble. A string is the delight of most birds, but it is dangerous, for they are apt to tangle it around their legs, and frighten if not hurt themselves; moreover, some birds will swallow a string, and suffer till they throw it up.

All this may be accomplished with a bird without making him what is called tame, *i. e.*, so much at home that he will come at your call, alight on you freely, take food from your lips, and let you stroke or handle him.

To make a bird tame, you should find out his special dainty, and reserve that to administer yourself. For a canary a hemp-seed is the great temptation; he never gets enough hemp-seed, because they are too rich for an exclusive diet. Take one in your fingers, and hold it close to the bars at the end of a perch, where he can approach on the inside and take it if he chooses. Then speak to him gently, or make a little chirruping sound or a low whistle. He may not take it the first time, and after you have held it there awhile, take it away. By no means drop it in his cage, or he will learn that by waiting patiently he will get it, whereas by taking it away he learns that he cannot have the hemp-seed till he takes it out of your hand. The second time he will be less afraid, and in a few days he will begin to tease for it.

With a soft-billed or insect-eating bird a meal-worm will work in the same way, and if you dislike to hold one of these wrigglers, a buzzing fly or a little spider will do as well. Either of these you may, if you prefer, hold in a pair of printers' tweezers with the same results. Gentleness and patience, and some

THE BOBOLINK

dainty the bird desires, will tame the wildest in time. Some birds are extravagantly fond of fruit—a berry, a soft-soaked currant, a bit of apple or pear; others prefer a morsel of fresh beef. Try your bird till you discover his choice, and keep that to win him with.

The old way of tiring out a bird, and refusing him any food or water till he takes it from the hand, seems to me unnecessary and cruel. When the victim at last snatches it because he is perishing for want of it, he is just as much afraid, and, besides that, he associates you with suffering and fear. The effect is the same as the parrot-taming above described. When coaxed with a tidbit, on the contrary, he is not suffering hunger; he has his common food; it is a luxury for which he is tempted to brave you. The effect is quite different.

If you let him out of the cage, you can easily teach him to come to your table or your hand for the coveted morsel, and if you are always gentle of voice and manner, he will rapidly lose his dread, and sometimes become troublesomely familiar, and— strange as persons who have not kept pet birds may think — a great deal of company for you.

To tame a bird completely, you must keep but one. These little fellows are very quick and strong in their feelings. If one really loves you, he will not tolerate a rival in your affections, and he will never be truly fond of you if you divide your attentions. Some birds are intensely jealous, not only of other birds, but of young children and babies. Indeed, to get his best out of one, either in affection, in intelligent acts, or in song, you must have him alone, and you will find that you must win his heart by love and kindness, just as you do bigger hearts about you. Once won, however, he is more loving and more constant than many people of your own size.

A bird and other animals, no less than a dog, will pine in the absence of the loved one, and will die from a harsh word. Cases of this kind have been authenticated too often to be ignored or denied. We deal with tender and loving hearts within these feathered frames, and we should be thoughtful and loving in our care. Above all, we should be gentle. Think what suffering our noisy ways must cause the delicately organized bird we forget upon its perch! The boisterous play or crying of children, loud talking or laughing, the roar of wagons on the pavement, the banging of a piano, or the rattle of a sewing-machine—each of these must cause nervous disturbance, if not positive pain, to a being so sensitive to the slightest sound.

There is a relation, beyond all these, possible to be established between birds and ourselves, which I have called "humanizing." It is similar to that so common between us and our pet dogs, and it changes the habits of the captive from bird ways to human ways. As our house-dogs learn to sleep on a mattress and be covered, to wear a protection from the weather, to wipe their feet, and other things, so the bird may be taught to sleep in a bed with his mistress, to eat from her dish at table, or be fed from a spoon, to consider her shoulder his proper perch, in fact to depend on her as a child would. This does not seem to me a healthy relation for the bird, and, as a matter of fact, it generally ends in unhappiness and death.

The reason is plain: to us it is a mere pastime, an amusement; to the bird it is the absorbing passion, a matter of life and death.

Few persons are willing to give to a pet for any long time the devoted and unremitting attention demanded by one whose feelings and emotions are cultivated beyond the natural relation between our race and the brute creation. It is far better never to go beyond "good comradeship" with our pets. Delightful friendships may be enjoyed within these limits, and more is almost sure to bring misery to the bird, and pain to those who love him. Among many other cases of unhappiness and death from excessive emotion in a "humanized" animal, I have known even so cold-blooded a creature as an alligator to show such absolute devotion to his mistress as to make her almost a prisoner with him, to cause him to pine in her absence, and end, most pathetically, in dying of joy on her return.

Why, indeed, should we wish to cultivate in what we call the lower orders, sentiments and emotions belonging to the higher? Few things are to me more pathetic than the appealing, yearning look in the eyes of an intelligent dog, who seems longing with all his soul for expression.

V

HIS PRIVATE APARTMENT

THE cage is the bird's private apartment, and to make him happy it must be as well suited to his needs, as comfortable and convenient, as our rooms are for us.

The first point to consider is the kind of cage to select. The indispensable quality, in my opinion, is that it shall be entirely of metal, without a particle of wood except the perches. The reason for this preference is that wood is hard to keep sweet and is a harbor for vermin, while cages of wire, with zinc trays, may be scalded and wiped dry in a moment. No insect can escape destruction, and there is no dampness or odor as from wet wood.

If but one or two birds are kept, and something very fine is desired, beautiful cages may be bought made of brass wire with zinc trays. These are rather costly, however, and if a cheaper one is decided upon, a very good plain cage in large sizes is made of iron wire, with suitable tray, and the whole painted, the upright wires one color, and the tin stays, of which there are three or four according to size, in a contrasting color. The best, and the most becoming to birds of whatever hue, is white for the upright wires, and some dark color for the stays and corner posts.

This cage has a wire bottom, which, when the tray and perches are removed, acts like a door with a hinge, and may be shut up within the cage. This arrangement makes it possible to pack the cages (which are made in three or four slightly differing sizes) in nests, which is a great convenience in putting them way. At the same time the wire bottom is a safeguard when the tray is removed to be cleaned. In every way I have found these cages most convenient.

The size is the next consideration. Dealers will tell you that to make a bird sing he must have a small cage. I have in my own house proved this to be a mistake. I never have a small one, and my birds sing as much as any one could desire. I should never put a bird, who was not to be let out every day, into a cage smaller than the conventional "robin cage" of the stores. Birds like large rooms, with space to flirt their draperies, as well as we do, and, what is almost as important, they do not wear off their feathers rubbing against the wires, as they do in cramped quarters.

> " 'Tis but a little rustic cage
> That holds a golden-winged canary,"

is poetical and pretty, but it is not practical, and to be practical is most important when we are arranging for the comfort of our captives.

When the cage I have described comes from the dealer, it usually has three small perches, one across each end just above the tray, and a third lengthwise, about half-way to the top. It will also be furnished with two small dishes fastened on the outside, and reached through a small opening in the wires.

To prepare it for use, the first thing is to remove the dishes; they are too small for any bird bigger than a canary, and are not readily found by any bird not born to cage life, and are troublesome to clean. Two new perches must be provided for the upper part of the cage. For these, which the bird uses most of

THE OWL

all, get two sizes of dowelling, one perhaps half an inch in diameter, the other three-quarters of an inch. Dowelling may be bought in three-foot lengths at house-furnishing stores in the city, and of carpenters in the country, and is convenient for several purposes in a bird-room. The two upper perches should be made of different sizes, to avoid cramps in the feet, which are caused by the use of perches too small, or all of one size. Fasten these in place by cutting a rather deep notch in each end.

Throw away the middle perch, and make another one of the dowelling, to go across half-way down, and exactly in the middle, coming thus over the door. Now these cages are somewhat elastic, and a notched perch will occasionally fall down from the middle of the cage, so this one must be fastened differently. I make it secure by cutting it square off, just long enough to fit loosely between the tin stays on which it is to rest, and driving straight into each end a large-headed tack, about two-thirds its length. When this is slipped into its place, the tacks rest on the strip of tin, and the heads keep it in.

Perches arranged thus, all the same way, across the cage, are more convenient for a bird, and a great pleasure also, as he will show by his constant use of them in all sorts of lively frolics.

The perches being placed, dishes for the bird's use must be procured. I prefer the open, straight-sided cups that are found in bird stores, about two inches in diameter and one and a half deep; but if a bird scatters his food, you will need another kind. The best is a dish of the size mentioned, with a flat cover, in which are three holes, perhaps three-quarters of an inch in diameter. The bird gets his food through the holes, while the cover prevents his scattering. This must, however, be watched, for if he eats mocking-bird food, he will dig a hole under each opening, and be unable to get more. You must look out that the cover is removed when the food gets too low, or turned a little, so that he can dig new holes. These two dishes should be placed in two corners of the cage, and so near the wires that they will not be under him in any of his ordinary positions on the perch.

It is a good plan, if the cage is over a carpet,

to keep the food from falling out by a screen, three inches high, of smooth white or buff paper woven between the wires, and extending four or five inches each way from the corner where the cup stands. If he inclines to spatter, get a deeper cup, shaped like a glass tumbler, perhaps one and a quarter inches in diameter. From this it is hard to throw anything.

These directions are for medium-sized and large birds; for a canary, or a bird of its inches, a dish outside, into which he must thrust his head, is not objectionable.

The tray should be covered with a quarter-inch or more of clean bird gravel, not a bit of paper with a little sand sprinkled on. It is important, too, to scatter over it something the bird is fond of; for a canary, or other seed-eater, a few hemp-seed; for an insect-eater, a meal-worm or a few berries. The object of this is to have the bird tramp around in the gravel, and so to keep his feet clean and in good condition. In the cage of a canary and other finches, should always be hung a piece of cuttle-fish bone.

The cage made ready, the next thing is to

decide where it shall be placed, and here one cannot be too particular. It must not be so near the window as to get the breeze that comes through cracks around it, and yet it should be near enough to enjoy the light these little fellows need. It must not be so low that the window can be opened directly upon the bird, nor so high that he will get all the hot air in the room. If the cage is small, and can be hung, put a bracket at one side of the window, so that he will hang near the casing, and several inches or a foot back from the glass. The best place is just above the middle of the window, with the crack between the sashes made tight in winter, either by pasting paper over it or calking it with the same. If there is no other window in the room, and that must be used for ventilation, it may be made safe by laying a closely folded towel or woollen cloth over the crack.

Always see that the shade is high enough to let the bird look out, yet be careful that he is not left to bake in the hot sunshine. If he must hang in the sun, always provide an awning for him.

If the cage is too large to hang, a bracket

may be put up for a shelf to rest on. One end should come up flush with the window-casing, so that the bird can look out. Whether there are a dozen cages in a room or only two, care must be taken that the upper perches of all are about the same height in the room. A bird nearly always sleeps on his upper perch, and he will be miserable if he sees another one higher than himself. I measure with a tape-line, and make all conform to the highest.

The cage must always be in the light part of the room, and near, as I have said, but not against, a window. It should neither be next to the heater to get hot air, nor near the floor to get cold air. About level with your own head when standing is a good height for a cage.

If you want your bird to go out in summer, hang the cage in the shade, and not against a house where the sun has heated it; a brick wall becomes like a hot stove after a few hours of beating sun, and a bird will suffer greatly if hung against it. He must never be set in the window to get the draught always there, but he may be hung below or one side of the window on the outside, if that side is shady. The

4

best place is under a piazza roof, or against the trunk of a tree, if no cats are about.

A bird that is let out is sometimes troublesome about getting into the cage of another, and insisting upon staying. To remove him without catching him, which it is always undesirable to do, take the food and water dishes from the cage he is in without startling him ; close the doors of all other cages except his own, in which put his dishes and any dainty he specially likes. He will soon get hungry, and leave the provisionless apartment, very likely flying to the top of his own. Here he can look down and see the feast spread, a temptation generally irresistible, and in a few minutes the door may be shut upon him.

I never had but one bird who would stay out and starve rather than go home, and that was a Brazilian cardinal. He did not appear at all discontented, and he seemed just as happy, when not let out at all; but once out, he had a rooted dislike to having a door shut upon him, and a vagabondish way of foraging upon his neighbors. He would stay contentedly in another bird's cage all day. When I wanted to get him home, I sat at my desk, with my back turned to him, with a small hand-glass in which I could see him. Yet even when I held his door-string in my hand, he would dash into his cage, snatch a morsel, and out again before I could slacken the string as gently as I wished, not to have the door close with a spring and startle him. Sometimes it required three hours of constant watching to get him home.

I could not bear to keep him shut up when others were out; it was not safe to let him stay out all night, and I could not give so much time to catching him. So, although he was interesting, I gave him away, where it was thought he could be out all the time. He was for a while, but he proved so exceedingly troublesome that at last he was shut in for good, and passed a happy summer in a cage on the piazza, carrying on music matches with bluebirds and robins, singing from morning till night, and apparently having just as good a time as when he was out every day.

A point that I consider important is that a bird shall have his cage to himself; it is none too commodious for him. Unless I have a pair, or two of the same kind, I never put two birds together. Even then I watch to see that one does not tyrannize over the other. Birds are surprisingly like people, and " love of rule " is by no means confined to our branch of the animal kingdom. If it is necessary to have two occupy the same cage, it should always be furnished with two sets of food and water dishes. That is the very least one can do for their comfort.

VI

WHAT SHALL HE EAT?

THE food of the caged bird is, naturally, one of the most important things to be considered, since his health, even his life, depends upon it. As already said, birds are divided into seed-eaters and insect-eaters, and it is much less trouble to take care of the former than the latter. In the selection of a pet, the question of the ability and the willingness to devote time to his care should largely govern the choice.

Of the birds mentioned in the chapter "Which Shall We Choose?" the following are the seed-eaters: All parrots and their tribes (cockatoos, love-birds, etc.); canaries, African and all other finches; the grosbeaks, cardinal and rose-breasted; the blackbirds; the Brazilian cardinals. To the soft-food eaters belong the mocking-bird, clarin, cat-bird, robin, and all thrushes; the orioles, bluebirds, tanagers, flickers, jays, and skylarks.

The canary, as is familiar to every one, and most of the seed-eaters as well, eat principally canary-seed with a little rape, and they should have hemp-seed for a dainty. Perhaps not every one knows that there is a great difference in canary-seed, and a bird will often refuse and scatter poor seed far and wide, while he will eagerly devour a better quality. The seed should be examined, and none used except that which is plump and large and clean. Seed should also be bought each kind by itself, and mixed at one's own discretion. It is the presence of a little hemp in the mixture of the bird stores that makes the bird throw seed all over the room. He is in search of what he likes best, the hemp, and so long as one of the large round tidbits is to be found in the dish, he will not touch the less acceptable canary.

Why not feed him entirely, then, on what he likes best? Because it is too rich. Would you feed your child exclusively on fruit cake or mince-pie because he will choose that from the dinner-table and refuse plainer food? The safe way is to scatter so much hemp as is safe for the bird on the gravel of the floor, perhaps a small half-teaspoonful for a canary and somewhat more for a larger bird. He will tramp around till he has found every one, and if he has not been totally demoralized by having these dainties mixed with his regular canary-seed in his dish, he will not try to find them by throwing everything out.

Now and then a bird thrives on hemp-seed exclusively, as some parrots and cockatoos, while others eat canary alone, as some cockatoos and several blackbirds. Still other finches, as the cardinal-grosbeak, live almost entirely upon "rough rice," or rice in the husk. They shell the grains very neatly, and they prefer them to the shelled rice of commerce.

No bird does so well on seed alone as when his bill of fare is varied by some sort of fresh food every day. At least such is the result of my experience with them, notwithstanding what bird-dealers and bird-books say on the subject. Without green food birds will suffer from constipation, while with it they are rarely afflicted in that way. There are many things of the sort that birds like, and each one has his individual taste, which must be consulted. Lettuce is a common luxury, and greedily eaten by many birds; but I have had several who would not touch it, while eagerly devouring sorrel or plantain. All of the following are good: chickweed, plantain (both seed stalk and young leaf), both sorts of sorrel, celery top, and lettuce.

Excepting the last two named, these may all be plucked between the sidewalk and the fence in every town where grass grows freely in the nooks and corners. In Brooklyn, for instance, one may easily keep any number of birds supplied. The way to place sorrel or any loose leaves in the cage is, after rinsing clean, to tie up a bunch of it, leaving long ends to the string, with which to fasten the bunch to the wires. By this arrangement a leaf may be plucked without throwing the whole on to the floor, where many birds will not touch it. Whatever is placed there should be secured so that it may be plucked and eaten without falling.

Many birds are fond of berries. Special favorites are huckleberries and "pokeberries;" a few birds like raspberries, several will eat cherries and grapes, and others like pears better than anything. In winter there are oranges, a section of which is a great treat to some birds, and bananas, of which a few are fond; but the great stand-bys of that season are apples and raisins and the dried currants of the grocers.

The apples we give to our birds should be well flavored and tender, such as one would put on her own table, and neither gnarly, sour, nor withered. A good apple cut into eighths, or even smaller, as one cuts it for pie, and wedged firmly into the cage directly over a perch, where the bird can get at it without clinging to the wires upsidedown, or hovering on wing before it, will generally make birds very happy. The currants should be washed, and soaked all night, when they will be full and soft, and a great treat to nearly all, especially to the soft-billed birds. Raisins must be cut into small bits and the seeds removed.

Another thing which would probably shock the bird-dealer, who has a regulation menu of " mixed seed " for all, is the fact, which I have proved to my own satisfaction, that nearly all seed-eating birds relish animal food, and are not hurt by a little of it. A meal - worm or two will be a treat to a grosbeak ; a few tiny snips, pin - head size, will be acceptable to smaller finches. Even the dainty orchard oriole in my house, who insisted on Bartlett pears for his daily bread, would pull to pieces and eat a meal-worm with great gusto.

The soft - billed birds have for their staple diet mocking-bird food mixed with an equal quantity of fresh grated carrot. The bird food should be carefully selected, for much of it that is sold has so offensive an odor that it is a wonder a sensitive bird will touch it. Some, indeed, will not, and they die of starvation with the uneatable stuff before them. The best is of a light gray color, free from odor, and almost as dry as loose sand. It contains ants' eggs instead of meat, and birds thrive on it. For readers who cannot get this food, I will give a receipt said to be good. A quantity of this may be made at once, and in a cool place will keep for months.

Mocking - bird Food. — One - half zwieback, one - quarter hemp - seed, one - quarter ants' eggs, with a little poppy or maw seed. All ingredients (except the ants' eggs) must be ground quite fine and thoroughly mixed. The ants' eggs added last.

The zwieback may be bought, or made by cutting into thin slices dry bread (free from alum or soda), and browning it in a very slow oven. The food must be freshly prepared with an equal quantity of grated raw carrot, every morning, and in hot weather twice a day, for it sours quickly, and no bird will eat sour food.

The soft-billed birds need also fresh animal food, or if they do not absolutely need it, they enjoy it very much. Meal-worms, which house-keepers know to their frequent disgust, three or four a day, will not hurt any bird, according to my experience, certainly not one fed on the food containing no meat, like that I have mentioned, and like the receipt. If these are not easily procured, fresh, sweet raw beef will answer the purpose. It may be cut into minute bits, pressed into a ball like a marble, and placed in a dish to keep out of the gravel; or, what I have found more convenient, it may be cut with scissors into strips the size of meal-worms, say an inch long, and as big as a common steel knitting-needle.

The same birds like ants' eggs, which may be bought at bird stores, and sometimes at drug stores. Half a teaspoonful of these should have very hot water poured on them and soaked till soft, then be put in a dish or on the bird's food for him to pick up. A bone with some bits of meat left on is a treasure to many birds, though it is somewhat unsightly in a house, and better fitted to be tied to a branch out-of-doors for the wild birds to enjoy. Food must always be fresh and of the best quality, or birds will not thrive.

It is almost impossible to keep from feeding parrots and other birds who are free about a house some of our food, and many of them show a great fondness for it. I know cockatoos who make a great row unless they have their morning coffee, and many of them eat of everything on the table, including hot doughnuts. But this diet is not good for them, and one day they will suddenly die, and no one suspect the cause. I have seen a parrot changed from a cross, bad-tempered fellow into a gentle, amiable bird, simply by having his diet limited to seed, and other things which he had been accustomed to eat denied him.

Raw green peas are a great delicacy for some of the larger birds, who take them out of the pod, then remove the shell of each pea, eating the inner part with great relish. They are not hurtful. Orange seeds are much liked by a cockatoo I know. He appears nearly wild whenever oranges are eaten in his presence, until the seeds are given to him, when he eagerly shells them, and eats every one. They do not appear to disagree with him. Within the limits defined, a bird should have as much variety as possible to keep him in health and spirits.

VII

HIS BATH

THE shape of an ordinary bird's bathing-dish, as sold in the shops, is one more proof of the universal thoughtlessness about the comfort of the beasts and birds whom we choose to have in our homes. It would be really funny, if it were not painful, to see how absolutely unfitted is the dish to its object. It could hardly be more inappropriate if it had been planned with that intention, and the only reason I can imagine for its present shape is the convenience of cage-makers. They have a notion that, to be symmetrical, the door of a cage should bear a certain proportion to the size of a cage, therefore everything that is to go in that door must conform. A round bath narrow enough to enter would be hardly larger than the bird's drinking-cup; but the dish may be lengthened *ad infinitum*, hence its absurd shape. It actually looks as if the dish-makers expected the bird to lie down in his bath as we do, and possibly that is their expectation.

The consequence of this blundering is that a cage bird scarcely ever enjoys a comfortable bath. If he is small enough to go in, his wings cannot touch the water, and it is with his wings that the bird sprinkles himself. More than this, the water is usually so deep for his length of leg that, to go in, his body must be in the water. Whoever has watched a wild bird bathing must have noticed that he goes in till the water comes not quite to his body, and then, with wings and tail spread, throws the shower over himself.

I believe that not one bird in a hundred will go into water deep enough to soak his body. One may stoop for an instant or two, and so let the water come up over him; but he will rarely stay long enough to wet the feathers through.

This inconvenience is the reason so many birds in our cages content themselves with scattering water with their head and beak only, and never go in. One often hears the complaint, "My bird will not bathe;" but I think almost every bird enjoys a bath, provided he has the conveniences for it. I have not found an exception to this in my bird-room, though I will say that I never kept parrots.

My discovery of what I consider the very best bird-bath was made by chance. The first bird I ever kept was an English goldfinch, which was given to me. This bird, as perhaps every one knows, is a little smaller than a canary. In trying to make him comfortable, the absurdity of the bath struck me, and I looked about for some more suitable dish. I tried several things, but not one was right until my eyes fell upon a saucer belonging to a common earthen flower-pot. It was about the size of a coffee-cup saucer, and, of course, somewhat rough. I tried this, and found it thick and perfect. Its thick edge enabled the bird to perch and hold on without trouble, its roughness prevented his slipping, its shallowness insured him against too great depth of water.

The delight of the bird, who had just come from the ship in which he had crossed the ocean, showed me that I had guessed right about his requirements. From that day to this no bird of mine has ever been obliged to bathe in a regular bird-bath.

Of course, this dish would not go through a cage door, and I had to take out the bottom of the cage, put the bath on a folded cloth or paper, and set the cage over it. The happiness of the bird amply paid me for this little trouble.

I think a bird's bath should be nearly as wide as the spread of his wings, so that he can indulge, as he does in freedom, in beating the water, and tossing it over him in spray. This is some trouble, to be sure; he must be placed where water drops will hurt nothing— in a bath-room, or on a table covered with oiled cloth or folds of linen or muslin to absorb the wet, and at a distance from furniture.

In my bird-room I had on the floor an oil-cloth six or seven feet square. On this stood the bathing-table covered with enamel cloth, with a thick towel laid over to absorb the greater part of the water. When bathing was over, the towel was always dripping wet, and the oil-cloth on the floor thickly spattered. The towel was wrung and hung to dry for next day's operations, and the oil-cloth dried in a moment by a floor-cloth or light mop. As before said, I think I never had a bird who did not delight in his "water privileges."

The flower-pot saucer is perfect, but it cannot always be procured. Sometimes it is not to be found large enough, and, again, florists do not like to sell them alone, and there is almost no retail sale of the pots. I have more than once bought a plant at a florist's solely to get the saucer for my birds. A further difficulty is that saucers large enough for birds the size of an oriole are rare, and one does not always want to buy a plant large enough to require it.

At last, when my need of more dishes became imperative, I looked about and found a substitute which answered the purpose nearly as well. This was the pressed-tin pie-plate sold by all house-furnishers or dealers in tin-ware. These plates come in all sizes, from six inches diameter—the smallest I ever use —up to ten or twelve. I got the deepest that come (which still are shallow compared to the china bird-baths), and those with a flat rim nearly half an inch wide.

The only objection to the tin dishes is their coldness in winter, but I obviated that by warming them a little over the register. To give them a little roughness like the earthenware, so that the bird's smooth claws shall have foothold, is important, because many birds are so frightened by the slipping and sliding of their feet on wet tin that they afterwards refuse to go in. I provided for this by a thick coat of oil paint, over which, while still wet, I sprinkled bird gravel. When the paint dried, enough gravel adhered to make it pleasantly rough. I used a dark color of paint because the birds were so attached to the earthen saucer, and I fancied they were not so timid about going in.

That my dishes suited their needs was abundantly proved by the eagerness with which they all bathed. Though I provided two and sometimes three dishes, there was more trouble about precedence at the bath than about any other one thing in the room.

An account of the bathing arrangement may be useful to persons who keep several birds. On the table, which was an ordinary folding cutting-table perhaps two feet by three in size, I placed two dishes with a standing perch between them. A bird does not like to fly directly to the bath, nor does he wish to alight on a table. He always prefers a perch, where he may pause to consider. To make one that should be portable and at the same time firm, so as not to tip over or even shake when an impetuous bird bounced on to it, was my problem, and this is what I made and have used for years:

I took a tin box, perhaps three inches high and four inches in diameter. Through the top of the cover at each end I punched a pair of holes, each pair being separated about an inch. Then across the top, so that it came between the two holes of each pair, I laid a rather large perch, and fastened it securely by passing copper wire through the holes and over the perch and twisting it tight on the under side. To make the whole thing firm and steady, I filled the tin box with pebbles, and then put on the tight-fitting cover with its foot-long perch. Of course this was made very wet every day, and had to be carefully wiped dry. This contrivance was also useful in many places in the bird-

THE BATH OUT-OF-DOORS

room. When the birds were accustomed to it, I could bring them to my desk or any table very easily by standing the familiar perch on it.

Sometimes it is desirable to give a bird the benefit of the large bathing-dish without letting him out of the cage; he may be new, or it may be that other birds disturb him. This can be done in either of two ways—the dish may be filled and placed on a table, then the bird's tray removed, and while his cage is held close over the dish, the wire bottom carefully drawn out, and the cage instantly set down over the dish. This operation cannot be safely performed with a bird liable to a panic, for he will be sure, in dashing about, to slip out of the cage while the wire bottom is half removed. If he sits quietly on an upper perch, it may be easily done.

In case of a timid bird the second way is best; he must have a bathing annex. To arrange this, put an empty cage on the table with the bathing-dish inside, remove all the perches, and fasten the door wide open. Then set the bird's own cage beside it, open his door wide, and place it against the open door of the bathing-cage so that he can go freely from one to the other. Then thrust a perch through the bird's cage and through the open doors, reaching to the bathing-dish. Then go away.

If the bird will not pass from his cage into the other, you can easily induce him to do so by covering his own cage with a dark-colored cloth. Tuck it in closely, so that his apartment will be dark, and the only light will come from the open door. He will very soon go to the light. Once in the bathing-cage, if you keep well out of the way, the wildest bird cannot resist bathing.

When he has finished, he looks at once for a perch, for the first instinct is to get up higher to dress his feathers. Then go quietly to the table, and gently and slowly draw off the cover from his cage. The sight of the familiar perches will soon draw him home to plume himself, when you can again come up carefully, and remove him and close his door. After getting accustomed to this routine, I have had birds that would come out and bathe on the open table with no cage over them, and return at once to their own cage.

The secret of this is to have no perch near except those in his cage. At the moment of leaving the bath, the bird's one idea is to dry his feathers, and if induced to return to the cage for that purpose, will, in the majority of cases, I think, continue to do so.

Even if my suggestions as to the size and shape of the bathing-dish are not adopted because of the trouble, I wish to urge upon bird keepers never to give a bird his bath on the gravel of his cage. It is sure to be dampened, and will grow musty and disagreeable, besides, in many cases, giving the bird a cold, which leads to suffering, if not to death. If he bathes in his cage, it should be over the empty tray; and when he has finished, the tray should be dried and dry gravel put on it. The drops of water should also be wiped from the wires of the cage.

If these things are systematized, and a convenient place provided for keeping all the implements and materials where they can be brought out and returned quickly, they will not be found much trouble, and will add greatly to the comfort as well as the health of the captive.

VIII

THE CANARY

ALL that I have said about the care of other
birds will apply as well to the canary, but this
bird is so common an inmate of our homes, and
so little understood and so frequently neglected, that I feel moved to give him a chapter to
himself.

The canary has been for so many generations a captive that he is almost as completely
domesticated as the chickens and ducks of
our barn-yards. More absolutely even than
they is he dependent upon us for his life, and
more trustfully than they does he nest and
raise his young under our very eyes. This
touching dependence and confidence should

make the "bird of the golden wing" very dear to us, and nothing should be left undone to make him as happy as a prisoner can be. Yet in many homes the bird in his gilded cage is hardly more than a piece of decoration ; he gets his seed, such as it happens to be, every morning (perhaps), and his water-cup is filled when his mistress happens to think of it; if he scatters his seed he is half smothered in muslin, and if he sings too much he is put in the dark ; but that he is a fellow-creature, with feelings, desires, and affections—that he needs companionship and love, never occurs to her.

To such pet keepers I have something to say.

First, the intelligence of the canary is very much underrated. So far from being a mere singing-machine, he has a character of marked individuality. He has his likes and dislikes as decided as our own, and not only has he a choice in the matter of food, place in the room, position of cage, and such things, but in his friendships with other birds, and between the members of the family.

Moreover, some canaries are good-tempered, gentle, and cheerful in disposition, while others are quarrelsome or sullen; one bird may be jealous to the point of fury, another pleasant and genial, and a third perfectly indifferent to every one. In a word, these birds show nearly all the passions of our own race, and one who would understand, and especially one who would teach them, must study their characteristics, and adapt the treatment to their peculiarities.

In the matter of mating, for example, a bird has his own notions, and must be allowed liberty of choice. Even the demure little damsels of canarydom accept or reject a wooer as they see fit. It is useless to insist upon union where there is disaffection; the result will surely be disastrous. Once united to their own satisfaction, a pair will remain mated for life, and if separated by a thoughtless owner will often mourn, and sometimes even die. Very touching stories are told of the recognition of a pair of birds when reunited after years of separation.

Not only have the birds a choice of companions; they are observing of their surroundings, and show decided preferences in colors as well as in positions. A bird will be unhappy or restless in one part of a room who will be perfectly contented in another, and I have heard of birds made miserable, and refusing to sing, by a peculiar wall-paper which they disliked, and of others who showed approval or disapproval of the color in their mistress's gown. I have spoken before of a bird's exceeding sensitiveness to unpleasant sounds and violence or abruptness of movement.

An English writer of many years' experience with canaries declares that most of their diseases are caused by terror, neglect, or cold. If this be true, and I firmly believe it, we should feel reproached as well as grieved over the illness of our little prisoners, for, as I have said before, no one has a right to take the happiness and the life of another being, even a bird, into her hands, unless she is able and willing to give intelligent and loving care to it.

As to the training of a bird, either to sing or to perform tricks, if that is desired, care should be taken to select one capable of learning; for there are great differences in ability as well as in docility. Some birds have naturally inferior voices, and on such ones time and labor will be wasted. Others again will be dull of comprehension, or sullen in disposition, and either not understand what is wanted or refuse to attempt it. Some, also, are not physically strong enough to endure the discipline of training.

To me it seems cruel to keep a bird in unnatural conditions of life, and then expect him to learn tricks and performances utterly foreign to bird nature, and if those who enjoy such exhibitions knew the torture and brutalities by means of which they are usually taught, I am sure a performing canary would be as painful a sight to them as it is to me. Of course the training to sing—if properly done—is quite different from other instruction, and I shall give in the next chapter some directions for that, from the best authorities.

To recapitulate: there are six things indispensable to the comfort of a canary:

First.—A cage large enough to give him exercise.

Second.— Regular attention; the best of canary-seed, with a little rape-seed, but no hemp in the dish; clean, fresh water every morning, clean perches and fresh gravel, with a little hemp-seed scattered over it. A little green food every day (when in health), such as lettuce, chickweed, apple, orange, or something else that he is fond of. Prompt and thoughtful care if he is ill. (See Chapter X.)

Third.—A proper position in the room ; near a window, but out of danger from draughts about it; neither too high nor too low (the bottom of the cage about five feet from the floor is best); not too near a register or radiator.

Fourth.—Protection at night if the room gets cool, such as a thin blanket wrapped closely around the cage, and secured below.

Fifth.—To be taken notice of, talked to, and recognized as one of the family.

Sixth.—To be treated gently; first, last, and always. All violence of tone or movement to be carefully avoided in his presence.

These rules, conscientiously carried out, will insure to a canary as happy a life as is possible to a bird who has no knowledge of liberty, either from experience or from inheritance.

IX

HIS MUSIC LESSON

To think of music lessons for a bird seems rather odd, for song is nature's gift to the feathered folk. Undoubtedly one hatched in solitude, and never allowed to hear the voices of his kind, would express his emotions in some sort of musical fashion. But, as a matter of fact, many, perhaps all, birds are taught to sing. I have myself heard several of them at what I believe to be their singing lessons, notably the American robin and the whip-poorwill. In both these cases the old bird sang his full song, and waited while the little one, with more or less success, imitated it. Over and over the parent repeated the notes, and the infant tried to copy them.

These are the native teachers, but birds destined to the life of parlor musicians, as the bullfinch and some others, have human teachers, when their music lessons are as regular as ours, and their instructors as painstaking as the professors who teach our daughters.

The canary is usually imitative and intelligent, and a wonderful capacity for song dwells within his tiny frame. I may say hers also, for his pretty little mate can sing, though not every one knows this.

There are three distinct ways in which a bird may receive a musical education. He may be taught to sing our tunes, opera airs or negro melodies, as is generally done with the bullfinch ; or, secondly, he may be instructed in the notes of another bird, as a lark or a robin ; or, thirdly, his capacity may be developed, his powers of voice cultivated, and his song remain the canary song through all.

The learning time in a canary's life is from five or six months old to a year, and the owner of one of these little fellows must make her choice of methods and begin in time. In the first place, she must see that her pupil is in robust health and good spirits. To insure that he shall have capacity, some persons recommend that he shall have peculiar training from the nest, to keep the muscular body flexible, since he cannot be taught to expand the chest by deep breathing.

A seed diet gives the muscles compactness; therefore, according to this system, seeds should not be the principal diet until he "graduates," but rather a soft food of hard-boiled egg grated with cracker or bread, and boiled in milk to the consistency of stiff paste. Some seed may be added, and this may be varied by bread and crackers in milk, and grated egg, or a little lean beef chopped very fine. He should have variety of food and plenty of it, for he is growing and must be well nourished. It is good, also, to let him fly about, for this helps to expand the chest.

Now to teach him. If he is to sing " Annie Laurie," or " The Last Rose of Summer," he must be placed in a quiet room, with the cage covered. Then a few notes of the chosen air should be whistled, or played on some instrument—flute, bird-organ, or piano. They must be played slowly and distinctly, in correct time, and over and over till the bird begins to try it himself. He must not see the teacher, nor hear the least noise to distract his attention from the notes so constantly repeated.

The instructor may have to spend hours, possibly twelve, before the bird learns his lesson; but he must persist in reiterating those few notes and no others, till the pupil repeats them. When he sings his notes he should be rewarded with something he likes; for one a bit of food, for another a little praise.

No matter how well he has learned his artificial song, he will forget it the first time he moults, unless it is carefully repeated to him every day while moulting.

If the bird's owner wishes the canary to sing like a lark or robin, he must be put under native instruction. He is to be placed, with his cage covered closely, in a room alone with his teacher, whose cage is in a light, sunny window. The lark sings for its own pleasure, and the canary, in his darkened cage, forced to pay attention to it, learns to imitate it.

One man, who kept a large number of canaries, tells of having one of them trained by a wild English robin. Her cage—for it was a female a year old—hung alone near the window, outside which was the robin's favorite singing-perch. The cage was uncovered, for

6

he never thought of training her, and for weeks she uttered no sound, but listened and looked at the singing bird, and one day she surprised her owner by giving the robin's song perfectly. Treated in the way described, a canary will learn to imitate almost any bird song.

The third method, and the most natural, is to have the young bird trained by a fine singer of his own family—a canary—and all that is needful to do is to keep the young one during the learning period in a room with the fine singer alone, when he will follow his copy so far as his powers allow.

The things to remember are that he should not be disturbed by other sounds, especially other singing, and that he learns more quickly if his cage is covered, so that his attention may not be distracted by seeing anything.

One caution should be heeded. However annoying or untimely a bird's song may be, he should never be stopped by violence, throwing something at him, scolding, or shaking the cage. These little creatures are exceedingly sensitive, and they are by terror sometimes thrown into an epileptic fit, and occasionally killed. If too noisy, his cage should be quietly covered, while a kind word is spoken to sweeten the imprisonment in darkness which he must suffer that his mistress may talk.

X

THE HOSPITAL

IT is a painful thing to see a bird unhappy or uncomfortable, and it is a real grief to see one ill. Even though you are not responsible for the bird's being in captivity, and have no neglect or carelessness to blame yourself for, you cannot help feeling reproached, and thinking you will never keep another.

There are three considerations in which I find comfort for the sickness and death of a bird. First, I did not cause him to be torn from his life of freedom and subjected to unnatural conditions; secondly, I have, in every case, bettered his lot, and spared no thought or labor to make him happy; lastly, my close study of birds has convinced me that Mother Nature is kind to her own, and that creatures who live natural lives do not suffer in illness and death as we do, who have so far departed from the simple, healthful, natural life.

Birds in illness do not seem to me to suffer, and I have watched them very carefully. They puff out their feathers, and act as if going to sleep, frequently burying their heads in the feathers for hours together. They appear dull, and not inclined to eat, but they do not act as if in pain, as a dog or other domestic animal does. When a bird has fits—a not uncommon trouble—he is undoubtedly unconscious, as are people similarly afflicted, and the struggle which is so painful to look at is merely muscular action.

The only way for a conscientious person to avoid self-reproach is to keep close watch of the little captives dependent upon him (or her), and try to attack the first symptoms of disorder. For example, fits are often, if not always, the result of an unhealthy state of the bowels, and if the bird had been closely looked after, some simple remedy would have set him right in the beginning. It is easy for an attentive observer to know the moment a bird is uneasy, and he should be attended to at once.

If a bird appears restless at bedtime, and tries to fly up through the top of his cage, one of two things is probably the matter—either he wants a cover on his cage, and a newspaper laid over will quiet him; or his upper perch is lower than some of his neighbors' perches, when his cage must be elevated to suit the requirements.

There are several common afflictions to which birds are subject, and I will give my method of treatment for them. First, let me beg the bird-lover never to submit her pet to the crude and often ignorant treatment of dealers, who proceed as if the poor victims were machines. Some of them will actually bleed a bird! Others dote on some special patent medicine, and drench the unfortunate with it, whatever may be the matter. There are books which coolly advise scraping the scales from the delicate legs and feet of a bird, and tell one to cut something out from under the tongue:—practice worthy of the Dark Ages we read about.

When anything at all is out of order in a bird, he should be at once put into the hospital—that is, removed to a quiet room, if possible, and if not, lightly covered up so as not to be disturbed. He should not be excited or annoyed in any way, and must be carefully watched.

Often a bird will mope on his perch, swelled out and motionless, eating nothing. The difficulty may be that he has swallowed a rubber band, a string, or something he cannot digest, and after an hour or so he will throw it up, matted into a little ball. If this ball is not at once removed from the cage, he will be sure to swallow it again, and have the whole process of discomfort and disgorging to repeat. A rubber band seems to be irresistible to all the thrush family. I suppose the elastic quality deceives them, and they consider it a worm. Whatever the reason, they cannot be cured of the habit of laboriously swallowing it, and as laboriously throwing it up again.

One of the first operations a bird-keeper may have to perform is cutting a bird's claws, which, unfortunately, grow so long in cage life that they catch on perch and wire, and endanger his legs and even his life. The bird should be caught as gently as possible, and something light, as a cambric handkerchief, thrown over his head, so that he may not see the formidable preparations. This operation needs two persons. One hand holds him gently but firmly, while the fingers of the other spread open the little drawn - up toes; another person must take a sharp pair of scissors, and cut each claw not nearer the toe than a long quarter of an inch.

If a bird chokes, a meal - worm or a bit of meat dipped in oil will often relieve him; he cannot resist the tempting morsel, and the oil helps the offending object to slip down.

When a bird takes to pulling out his feathers, try giving him raw beef or meal-worms; it is said to be the desire for animal food that causes this.

If the feathers are slow to fall out during moulting time, fresh pokeberries in the cage are recommended. A great deal is said in bird books about troubles in moulting, but it is my experience that a bird kept well, having a daily variety of food, and, above all, made happy and interested in life, will have no trouble at all in going through this process. Nature takes care of that. I never had the smallest occasion for tonics or other remedies. My birds are sometimes rather quiet, but they never lose spirits or appetite. Indeed, I should hardly know when it occurs but for finding the dropped feathers in the cage.

If your bird mopes and seems miserable in moulting, exert yourself to divert him; try some way to give him happiness and a fresh interest in life, and I believe you will find this a charm above medicine.

Cold is perhaps the most common disorder of birds, caused, in general, by the carelessness of their owners. A cold is indicated by sneezing and coughing, and the patient should be treated like a human being — removed from draughts, kept quiet, and given medicine.

The only medicine one should dare administer to a creature so delicate as a bird is the homœopathic, and I have found Humphrey's Specifics the most simple in cases like this, where the little sufferer cannot tell how he feels. In the case mentioned, take the Specific for a cold, and dissolve one pill in fresh water in the bird's drinking-cup. Then every time he drinks he will take his medicine.

A domestic remedy for a cold, which is sometimes successful, is a piece of raw salt pork fastened between the wires. The bird will peck at it, and I have known it to cure aggravated cases of long standing, where the patient had lost his voice, and experienced great difficulty in breathing. I have, however, found the Specifics unfailing in cases of this kind.

If your bird seems feverish, i. e., drinks often, but does not eat, proceed in the same way, using the Fever Specific.

Looseness and binding of the bowels are treated exactly the same way—that is, by using the proper Specific — remembering, however, that in the former trouble green food should be taken away, and in the latter more should be supplied. In the case of looseness, a rusty nail in the drinking-cup is thought to be useful, and, if he will eat it, boiled milk and bread. In bad cases of constipation a drop of oil is sometimes very desirable, and it can be easily administered without scaring him into fits by catching him and thrusting it down his throat, as is generally recommended.

This is the way: take a small glass medicine-dropper, and draw into it a drop or two of the oil you wish to give, which I hope I need not say should be of the same kind you would give a child. Holding the oil at the end of the tube, thrust the point of it towards the bird. In nine out of ten cases (if not in all) he will come at it with open mouth, to scold or to fight it, and the moment he gets near enough, press the bulb, and send the oil down his throat.

In the same way may be administered a dry powder which is a specific for sore throat, more especially a diphtheritic sore throat. This powder is iodide of mercury, and it may be got of the proper strength at a homœopathic pharmacy. Of course for this use you must have a perfectly dry tube, and you can proceed in the way already described, giving him a slight dash of the powder over his sore throat. In any trouble of the throat, he should be fed with soft food, like bread soaked in milk, or grated boiled egg, or mashed potato (without butter).

If the bird is restless at night, and moves about on his perch, he is probably troubled by some sort of insect pest. To remedy this, first scald every perch in his cage, especially on the ends, which you may then sprinkle with insect powder, treating his cuttle-fish bone (if he has one) in the same way. Wash the cage also in scalding suds made from carbolic soap. This will settle most of the torments; but if the bird is still suffering, take him in your hand, and retire to the bathroom; hold him over a bath-tub or a bowl of water; gently lift one wing after the other and throw under it, from an insect-powder gun, a goodly supply of Persian insect powder. Try to send it under and among all his feathers while you hold him loosely.

Before you have finished you may find your hand covered with his minute tormentors, while the water in the bowl is liberally sprinkled with them. Then let him loose at once in a cage you do not use. He will flutter and beat his wings, and sometimes shake out thousands of the enemy. I was never more astounded than at the numbers that deserted a flicker in my possession when treated thus.

When he seems relieved, put him back into his own thoroughly cleaned cage, and plunge the temporary one into scalding suds for its purification. This will always, I think, put an end to his misery.

In any disease that you can diagnose administer the proper Specific. For example, a

bird, especially an old one, sometimes seems
to have rheumatism. The books will tell you
to soak his feet, but think how you must
frighten him to hold his feet in water long
enough to have any effect! If the cage were
put into water and perches removed, as sometimes recommended, any bird I ever saw
would at once fly to the wires for safety, and
cling there till he dropped from fatigue. In
either of these two ways I think the fright
and excitement would undo any good from
the soaking. The only way I should treat it
is with the Specific, and keeping him in a
warm place, out of draughts and dampness.
It is said that bryonia and colchicum (homœopathic) in alternation will cure this disease.
To give medicines in this way you need two
drinking - cups prepared with the remedies :
leave one cup in his cage an hour, or until
you see him drink; then remove it, and substitute the other.

There remains to speak of the most troublesome disease that attacks a cage bird, and one
usually considered incurable. I refer to fits.
A close observer, as I have said, need never
have to deal with this trouble if she will at-

tend to the first symptom, for fits result, I believe, almost always, from days or weeks of
constipated bowels.

If, however, the little sufferer does get so
far, and his friend makes up her mind to devote a day or two to him, she can cure him.
First, the gravel must be removed from his
tray, and several thicknesses of soft old muslin substituted, so that he will not be hurt,
nor get dirt in his eyes, if he does fall. Then
medicines for the difficulty should be fixed in
his water-cup, and the cage set down on the
table close at hand, where you can reach him
without moving. Next, you must provide
yourself with a small sponge saturated with
ether or chloroform, with a tight - covered
china, glass, or tin box in which to keep it.

Do not read or sew and forget the bird, but
look at him every few minutes. If he begins
to reel on his perch and act as if he would
fall, snatch the sponge out of its box, thrust
your hand into the cage, and hold it under his
beak. It will act like a charm; he will stop
reeling, and stand steadily, looking a little
dazed. Then the danger is over for that time;
replace the sponge, and wait again. You may

have to do this two or three times an hour for a day, or even two or three days; but if by this time you have cured the exciting cause with the medicine you are giving, your bird will recover.

He will probably be too weak to go down for food. I have treated a bird thus for three days, and fed him myself by holding his food dish up to him where he sat, on the upper perch, afraid to go down. He would eat all he wanted, and then I held the water and let him drink. He took kindly to being nursed, and from a very wild bird he became perfectly tame under my care.

If a bird is contented on a low perch, it is best to take out all the upper perches; but some birds would be very unhappy under these circumstances, and you must carefully avoid making him discontented or disturbing him in any way.

While under treatment it is important to keep a bird warm, quiet, and rather dark. Nature alone is a good nurse, and observing the above conditions, with a wholesome "letting alone," will frequently bring a bird as well as a beast back to health.

XI

THE TALKING TRIBES

THE parrot is, next to the canary, the most general favorite as a cage bird. Perhaps if he cost no more than his yellow-coated rival, he would take the lead. He is so important a member of our households, and there is so great ignorance as to his character and abilities, as well as to his care and requirements, that he must have a chapter to himself.

No one should buy a parrot who is not personally fond of birds, and prepared to adopt him as an intelligent member of the family, demanding not only seed and water, but love and attention.

All the parrot family are birds of the finest organization, susceptible to affection or neglect, capable of being either charming companions or unmitigated torments. They are endowed with strong emotions, and suffer from the same passions that we do; they feel love and jealousy, as well as hate and rage. They often die from strong emotion, some fright or fury, grief caused by rough words or scolding of a friend, or of longing for an absent loved one.

A bird left to the care and society of servants, or one considered merely as an ornament, lives a joyless and wretched life, almost as would a child under similar treatment. It is necessary to his well-being that he shall love some one. Without this his talents develop in every unpleasing way; he learns not to talk, but to scream, to bark like a dog, to whistle like the boys in the street, to imitate the city cries, or the coughing of an old man. In a word, he becomes a nuisance in a house; and he is not to be blamed for it.

It is unfortunate that we cannot begin the training of our parrot; as it is, he has learned many things before he comes to us, and the first lesson is usually the unlearning of the teaching he has had. Many a bird has a ruined temper, with habits of screaming and using bad language, firmly fixed before he goes into a family. These habits it is difficult and sometimes impossible to break up.

When the love of an intelligent parrot is really won, no bird can give so much satisfaction as a pet. But he must be first tamed, then won, then taught; his bad habits must be corrected; his health must be established.

To accomplish all this requires care and patience, as well as a knowledge of the best method of treatment.

Begin with his taming. If you take a bird from a dealer, you will probably find at once that he is not friendly; he will either be frightened, and squawk or scream when you come near him, or he will show temper, scold, and try to bite.

Your first step is to convince him that you are his friend, that you will neither tease nor hurt him. This is to be done, first, last, and all the time, as with other pets, by gentleness, quiet ways, and unvarying kindness. If you indulge in any violence in the room with a parrot, if you speak loud or sharply, whether to him or to any one else, if you tease him, if you "fly at him," bang his door or your own, or if you allow any one to do these things, you will never have a gentle, pleasing house-mate.

I think it will be found that the tamest, most sweet-tempered parrots belong to gentle women in houses where there are no children and no men; for it is a singular fact, which I do not attempt to explain, that not only boys, but the majority of men, delight in teasing or "bothering" a bird. It is generally done in sport, but our play is too clumsy for him, and his temper is almost certain to be spoiled. It is a valuable rule to make, and strictly enforce, that your bird—especially your parrot—shall never be teased.

Next in importance is to see that the wants of your captive are carefully looked after, his cage kept clean and sweet, his food fresh and of the best quality, his water-dish properly replenished. Go no further than this for a week or two, or until he gets used to his new surroundings and shows less fear of you, and, if possible, keep him in a dark room away from the family gathering-place.

Then begin your personal wooing; talk to him quietly; offer him some dainty to eat, or some trifle to play with, a fresh twig to gnaw, or a cracker to nibble. When he is calm and attentive to you, try—cautiously at first—to rub the top of his head with one finger thrust between the wires, by no means putting your hand in the cage. If he draws away, give it up at once ; never press the point.

I have, in a previous chapter, spoken of taming a parrot by force, but it is a misuse of terms to call it taming ; it is, in fact, subduing by fatigue and hunger. The victim of this treatment is never anything but slavishly obedient, and differs radically from the bird who is won and tamed by patience and gentleness.

If you can give a good deal of time and thought to it, this important taming may be hastened by placing the cage close to your seat, a little lower than your face. The cage for this purpose should be rather small, so that he has not much freedom of motion. Then all the arts of winning above spoken of should be employed, when the captive, with attention concentrated on that one thing, will sooner be conquered.

After he is thoroughly convinced of your friendship, and no longer shrinks from you, nor shrieks when you approach, begin to teach him ; for he is like a child : if not learning something good, he will be picking up some-

thing bad. First, let me beg you to rid yourself of the old false notion that anything about
the tongue must be cut; it is as unnecessary
as it is cruel.

It is said a parrot will learn most easily from
a woman's voice, and he is taught exactly as a
child is taught, by repeating the desired word,
slowly and distinctly, just as you want him to
say it. It is best to begin with one word, and
that perhaps most natural is his own name.
I hope it will not be " Polly," and I protest
against his first sentence being the traditional
request for a cracker. There are already thousands if not millions of parrots in the world
dinning that sentence into our ears; let us
have something original, or at least fresh.

Take care also in teaching a word that the
bird understands it. If you give him a nut,
say " Nut;" when you come in, say " Good-
morning;" when you go out, say " Good-bye."
In this way you will have a bird who knows
what he is talking about, instead of one who
rattles off remarks like a string of phrases in a
foreign language. Do not fancy that the bird
attaches no meaning to the words; to him I
believe they always mean some definite thing;

but if you have not taken pains to have him understand what they mean to you, he may not use them as you do. For instance, if you teach him the senseless "Polly wants a cracker," without showing him, by offering a cracker, what is meant, he may understand it to be a mere greeting, like "Good-morning;" and I believe many birds say this without in any way connecting the idea of a cracker with it.

No one who has lived for any length of time in the house with a parrot has any doubts of its sagacity or understanding. To say that the bird does not mean anything by his remarks is seriously to underrate his intelligence. Moreover, thousands of instances could be collected, of parrots combining words in new ways, and plainly showing that they understand them. I heard of a case not long ago of a parrot deeply attached to a young lady who died away from home. Soon after the event the bird began to call, " Where's Alice?" and to ask the question of the family, and every guest who came in. He had never done it before, and it harrowed the grief-stricken household to such an extent that the bird was punished for it. He readily understood what was his offence, and did not repeat it to the family. But—here comes the proof of his intelligence—when a servant or stranger was in the room alone, he would lean forward eagerly, and in a sepulchral whisper propound his anxious query, " Where's Alice ?"

Another proof is furnished by a bird exceedingly fond of one of the household, whom he called " Mamma." On one occasion she felt obliged to reprove him ; she spoke severely to him, and threatened him with a little stick, though she did not touch him. From that moment he was alienated ; he no longer called her by the tender name ; he was cross to her, and even to her children, whom he distinguished from their cousins in the same house. It was months afterwards when she told the story, and though she had made every effort, he still refused to be won back; he would not forgive.

Stories of this bird's intelligence are innumerable. Every parrot owner has a stock of them, and one could easily collect enough to fill many books. It is well known that parrots are as capricious as human beings in their likes and dislikes; but it is not so generally understood that they are also stronger in their attachments, for, having fewer objects to interest them, they set their whole heart on one they love.

To break a bird of a bad habit or of using an offensive sentence is hard, but it may often be done by persistent effort and never-changing kindness. Perfect content and happiness, and a good deal of attention in the way of being talked to and amused, will generally break up the habit of screaming, which is frequently acquired from the confusion in a bird store, where every one tries to out-shriek his neighbor, or may be the result of loneliness or an unoccupied mind.

If he is to be cured of any trick, it must never be laughed at. Some people will laugh at the naughty doings of a child or a parrot, which at the same time they wish to correct. As with a child, laughing at it is fatal to the hope of curing it. The bird understands as well as the baby that it is a funny or a smart thing to do or say, and the task of the trainer is thereby made much harder.

Better than to laugh or take much notice of it, is to divert the bird by something interest-

ing, present something to him, or talk to him;
make him forget it if possible. It is said that
a green parrot given to screaming can never
be entirely cured, while a gray one may be
made to forget it absolutely. An unmanageable, screaming bird can rarely be taught anything.

Do not forget that a parrot dislikes inno-
vations, and generally becomes silent when
moved to new quarters or cared for by new
hands. That is why a bird fresh from the
store often appears to be dumb.

A great help in the training of a parrot is
to place his cage beside that of a talking bird.
These little creatures will not only learn more
readily from each other, but they have ways
of imparting their own impressions to strange
birds; you may decide for yourself in what
manner, but those who know them best declare it is by conversation.

The health of a bird is a most important
consideration, for all the taming and training
is wasted if the object of it is in poor condition
or dies.

The first great mistake of a parrot keeper is
in feeding it from the family table. There is

a certain fascination in seeing a bird eat bread and meat, and drink coffee and tea, irresistible to many persons; no creature takes more kindly to a human diet than a parrot, and to none is it more often fatal. Sometimes, it is true, a bird will live years under this treatment, either because the family menu is not over-rich, or because the bird has a stronger constitution than most of his kind; but, in the majority of cases, it causes illness, shown by bad temper and fretfulness — before long by death.

To avoid the begging of a parrot, and the temptation to yield, it is always best to keep the bird out of the dining-room, for nothing is harder than to refuse the plain request of a captive.

The best food for the gray, and the green about his size, is simply dry corn or seed— hemp, canary, or millet—with plain tepid water to drink. Crackers will not hurt him, but if he have any bread, it should be dry. Smaller parrots and paroquets should have very little or no hemp, which is too rich. Green food is said to be unnecessary to parrots; but I think a little fruit, perfectly ripe, or green corn or green pease, occasionally given to a thoroughly acclimated bird, will do no harm, and will be a treat he will greatly enjoy. Nuts—hazel-nuts, almonds, and walnuts —are not bad for him; fresh twigs to nibble at are desirable; sparingly at first, and always soft wood, like willow, poplar, birch, or fruit tree.

All food must be good and fresh, and in winter not just out of a cold room, and so of an icy temperature. There should always be a bit of cuttle - fish bone fastened in the cage.

There is a curious notion abroad that this bird does not need water. It is a fact that he can live a long time without it, but it is cruel to deprive an acclimated bird, and he does not flourish so well without it. The case of a bird freshly imported is somewhat different. Of such I shall speak later. A parrot, as well as other birds, should always have plenty of gravel or sand on the bottom of his cage.

In regard to bathing there is great variety of opinion. It is a fact, I believe, that the gray African parrot and the green ones of his size will never bathe in a cage; but many of them show great delight at being sprinkled,

and all of them need it now and then for
health. It is customary to bathe a parrot by
putting him, in his cage or out, according to
his degree of tameness, into a bath-tub or
basin, spraying him with lukewarm water from
a hose sprinkler or a watering-pot, and keeping him in a warm room for several hours.
Most birds like this sort of shower-bath as
often as once a fortnight. Another way is to
dip a leafy branch in water, and hang it in
his cage, where he can rub against it. Most
of them enjoy this arrangement thoroughly;
it probably approaches their native way of
bathing.

The position of the cage is no less important with this than with other birds, and the
subject has been fully treated in a former
chapter. The parrot, being a tropical bird,
must be carefully guarded against cold, never
taken into a cold room, and snugly covered
on cold nights, or you will hear him

> "sneeze or cough·
> All his red and green and gold
> Cannot fright away the cold,
>   Cannot keep the winter off.
> Ruffled feathers, rough and dim,
> Tell Jack Frost hath bitten him."

In regard to the treatment of this bird in illness, I should do with him exactly as I have described with other birds.

Some particular directions are necessary in the care of birds newly imported. It is safer to buy one already acclimated, but it is not difficult to acclimate one if a person knows how, and will take the necessary pains. The conditions under which the bird has been brought from his distant home are peculiar, and he must be gradually accustomed to different ones.

To begin with, he has made his voyage entirely without water, and he must be inured to the use of it by a few swallows a day, steadily increased till he can be trusted with an unlimited supply. (I am supposing your bird has been imported in the ordinary way. If he came as a sailor's pet it will be different.)

The change of food is always great, and usually brings on the disease of which most of them die—viz., dysentery. A simple and sure cure for this is lime-water, in connection with warmth and perfect quiet. In buying, you should always find out what a parrot has been fed on, and gradually change, if change is desirable, to the food preferred. No fruit, or green food of any description, should be given to a newly-arrived bird.

If your bird has black eyes he is young, in spite of his venerable appearance and manners. He must, it is said, be fed for a time on corn that has been chewed by his keeper, as that is the diet he gets from the sailors; but this should be inquired into when buying one.

One thing must not be forgotten: neither parrot nor cockatoo is a safe companion for other cage birds, or for birds at liberty in the room with them. There seems to be war to the knife on the part of the parrot family towards all the smaller tribes of its kind.

The cockatoo belongs to the parrot family in the books, but in several respects he is quite different from the parrots. He is a more beautiful bird, being, as we find him in the cage, either snowy white, with lemon or sulphur color in his elegant crest, or of a delicate rose-pink hue. There are rare species who dress in black, but not one wears the gay and often glaring colors of the parrots.

Then, again, he is an affectionate fellow.

While a parrot will live in health and good spirits for years in a home where he is not particularly loved or cherished, a cockatoo must be the object of affection, or he will grow ill-tempered, or mope and die. He must love, or be at war with his neighbors.

Another difference is in liveliness of temperament. No bird is more grave and dignified than a parrot, while the cockatoo is of a rollicking humor, with quaint and droll ways that make him a lively and amusing companion. When he is happy, and feels himself thoroughly at home, a cockatoo is full of play; he bows and postures, lifts his feathers in comical ways, lies on his back and plays with a stick, turns somersaults, and performs many entertaining gambols. It is delightful to see two cockatoos amuse each other with their funny antics, sometimes rolling over together on the floor like two kittens.

In intelligence the cockatoo is remarkable even in this celebrated family. His admirers say that he will be found to excel even the dog in this quality. He attains this development, however, only in cases where he is loved, and treated as a companion from whom sagacity and understanding are expected. No bird is more influenced by his affections. In the warmth of love and appreciation he expands like a flower in the sunshine, and becomes almost painfully knowing; while in the atmosphere of coolness or indifference he is reserved and self-contained—to carry out the figure—as a bud which has never opened.

A beautiful cockatoo lived in a certain house that I visit. He was not particularly loved; the child to whom he belonged teased him, and the mother, who took care of the bird, had frequent occasion to reprove him, for he had some disagreeable tricks, such as squawking, scattering his food and water, getting out of the cage and destroying things. As time went on he was given away, where he fell into the hands of a real pet lover, and was at once made a member of the family, and loved and petted. He soon became a different bird, gentle, affectionate, and most amusing. His naughty pranks seemed forgotten, and squawking he left off entirely.

This susceptibility to varying conditions is so strong an indication of intelligence that even the extreme statement of his lovers in

THE COCKATOO

regard to his superiority to the dog cannot be gainsaid.

Sometimes a cockatoo, while gentle and loving with one, is absolutely savage with others, scolding and biting strangers, or those from whom he has received slights or annoyance. Indeed, the memory of this bird for what he regards as injuries or offences is phenomenal; he really seems never to forget.

Again, the parrot is not generally an active personage; he will often stand on a perch or sit in a cage all day, and apparently make no effort to change his place or to entertain himself; while, on the contrary, the cockatoo will investigate every part of his quarters, opening his door if it is not locked and the key removed, showing a cleverness in the use of his beak that is simply amazing.

But the cockatoo rarely talks; he has so extensive a *répertoire* of expressions that he seems not to need the spoken word. He will generally speak a word or two, sometimes a sentence, and I have heard of accomplished talkers; but in this respect he cannot compete with his parrot relatives.

The health of the cockatoo requires as careful supervision as that of the parrot. He should not have soft food, though he likes it. He should eat hemp-seed or dry corn; if any bread is allowed, it must be well baked and dry. Ship's biscuit or any plain cracker will not hurt him.

There seems to be no regular time for moulting with these birds when in the cage. Indeed, some of them go for years without change of plumage. They may be rather quiet during that period, and should have particular care about temperature and proper food; but if they are kept all the time in good health, I do not think they will be ill while passing through that natural process.

There are several other birds who come under the head of "Talkers," of whom I will speak next. There is first the starling, a beautiful bird of dark bluish-green—so dark that at a little distance it seems black, with dainty tips of buff and pale brown. He is a European bird, easily tamed, and capable of talking nearly, if not quite, as well as a parrot. An English lady who has brought up two of this family writes most enthusiastically of their intelligence and charming qualities as pets.

The magpie is another talker, and an exceedingly busy and entertaining bird besides —that is, if one has plenty of room for the exercise of his abilities; for he develops best outside a cage, and is without doubt the most mischievous bird we have.

The common crow will learn to talk, and another of his family, the raven, is really a fine linguist, learning very rapidly, and rarely forgetting any sentence he has once mastered. He has also, like the parrot, the advantage of long life to repay one for the trouble of teaching him. But he is another too active to keep in a cage, and too large and full of mischief to be an altogether agreeable house-mate.

The mino, a native of India, frequently to be found in our bird stores, is another talker and an interesting fellow, being intelligent as well as affectionate. He speaks readily, but the disadvantage with him as a cage bird is that his native calls seem to be all shrieks, and he is so fond of uttering them at the top of his voice that few persons can endure him in a house; and hung outside, he becomes a nuisance to a neighborhood. It is probable, however, that if he had some liberty, and therefore some ways of amusing himself, he would not show such a passion for screaming.

XII

THE BIRD-ROOM

A SUNNY outlook and plenty of windows are indispensable to a successful bird-room; next in importance is an even temperature through the day, without too great change at night; lastly, thorough ventilation without draughts. These conditions granted, a bird lover may set up her (or his) little colony, with assurance of being able to make its members happy and contented. She must, however, be devoted; much time and earnest thought are required to keep a feathered family in health and spirits.

To prepare the room: There must be no carpet on the floor to harbor dust and clog their little lungs with wool fibres, no upholstered furniture to be injured, no delicate bureau coverings to be mussed, no tidies and table scarfs to be soiled; no knick-knacks whatever. In one word, everything within the four walls must be free to the birds, or they will not feel at home and act naturally.

If the bird-room is also the study, folded newspapers may be laid over the tops of standing rows of books, none of which should be left out of place. Boxes and drawers must be at hand to hold everything one wishes to preserve. Table-tops should be left bare, so that they may be wiped off; straw matting, which can be scrubbed (if needed), must cover the floor. Then, with no danger of their hurting anything, birds are free to do whatever they like, the only conditions under which they will be natural and interesting.

The windows of the bird-room should be protected by screens or inside blinds, so that in mild weather the lower half may be open for air, while the upper half lets in sun and light. There are only two birds that I know, the size of a canary or larger, who will pass between the slats of a blind; birds rarely go where they cannot fly through. But the two orioles—the Baltimore and the orchard—will creep through any opening, so that nothing less than screens are safe for them.

By inside blinds I do not mean the useless things usually found in a house, divided into unsteady, unmanageable sections, part of which are panels, and with slats so small and near together that they keep out everything, including fresh air; I mean a good, firm blind, the size of the lower sash of the window, made to order in one piece, to be put into the open window like a screen, bolted to place with tiny brass bolts, and having slats of good size extending at least half their width. Such blinds as these, of oiled pine, I have had made for one dollar a window, and they were an unspeakable comfort, letting in plenty of air, and keeping the birds as safely as the smothering wire gauze.

No draperies or curtains are allowed in a bird-room, to gather dust or trap the birds to their death, as I have known them to do. The windows should have shades, to the bottom of which may be lightly sewed a piece of unwashed white mosquito-netting or coarse lace, the length and width of the window. This supplementary shade may be neatly folded up and pinned to the ordinary shade, being invisible from the outside; or it may be dropped to form a gauzy veil over the whole window. This should be done when a new bird is let out of the cage. If only the broad, clear panes are between him and the out-of-doors, he is sure to fly against them, expecting to get out. Until he learns the nature of glass—which he soon does—it is well to employ the lace shade.

Cages must be all near the windows. I had in my bird-room three bookcases about four and a half feet high; one stood between the windows, and one against the wall each side, next to the windows. On the top of each of these cases I fastened a broad board shelf to hold the cages. There were two cages between the windows, two on each shelf at the sides of the room, and two or three hanging on brackets. By this arrangement I made comfortable quarters for six large cages and two or three smaller ones, each near a window. Cages, even the largest, may be hung on strong nails or hooks in the wall, but a shelf is better.

Behind the shelves, to protect the paper from spatterings, I fastened, with common pins, sheets of buff wrapping-paper, which I bought by the quire to have it smooth and fresh. As they became soiled, perhaps after a month, I replaced them with new ones.

Each cage had, in addition to its full complement of perches, one piece of dowelling, at least two feet long, which I called a door perch. When I opened a cage door to let out its occupant, I thrust this perch through the door, and wedged it tightly between the wires at the back. Thus it ran completely across the cage, and projected a foot or more into the room. The bird ran out on it, and alighted on it in coming back. It is hard for a bird to learn to fly directly into his door, and the process of getting home is greatly simplified if he can fly to a perch and run in.

In the room I put up numerous perching-places, so that birds need not alight on chairs and other furniture. They will rarely do this if provided with convenient places in the lightest part of the room.

For my little family I arranged them thus: Across, in front of each window, reaching from the cage on one side to that on the other, I fastened a long perch, thrusting it firmly in between the wires; sometimes I had one run from a cage to the top of a lower sash of the window, resting against the casing. I was careful to make it firm always, for birds do not like a shaky perch, though they enjoy a swinging one. From a cage on the side of the room to another which was between the windows or across the corner, I fixed perches perhaps six feet long. For these I used strips of lancewood that comes for fishing-rods (having a fisherman in the family). Slender bamboo poles would do as well, or better, but dowelling does not come long enough.

Between a gas-fixture and a cage I fastened another, lashing it with twine to the fixture, to have it steady. In one bird-room, where an alcove was defined by an arch, I had stretched across from the tops of an ornamental projection on the arch a perch six feet long, made of "printer's furniture." These were inch-square strips of pine about three feet in length, which were spliced together. Under this perch I hung by wire loops a piece of dowelling for a swing, which pleased the birds greatly.

As part of my furnishings—all of which, by-the-way, were evolved one by one as the need appeared—I had two ladders, which I made by lashing thin rounds of printer's furniture (about the size of the stick at the bottom of a window-shade) with fine twine on to two long strips of lancewood. These ladders were nearly six feet long, and reached from the floor to the door of any cage whose occupant was unable to fly because of moulting, or from any accident. The rounds were eight inches apart, and it was a pretty sight, when a disabled bird had fallen to the floor, to watch him hurrying across the room, and hopping up the rounds of that ladder as fast as a child will run up-stairs. Birds learned to use them very readily.

Most of the cages were left uncovered; but birds who were sensitive about having others alight on their roof had their cages covered. Usually a newspaper laid over answered the purpose; but in one case of an extremely nervous bird and a very teasing neighbor, I sewed a permanent roof of enamelled cloth over the top, making the lovely owner thereof perfectly happy.

Before one of the windows of the bird-room stood the table, which served first every morning as a place to put the cages to rights, and later as a bathing apartment for the residents. The daily routine of the room was this : After my breakfast I brought out from a cupboard devoted to the birds' belongings a coarse grater, a clean newspaper, a box of mocking-bird food, a carrot, and a silver knife. Sitting down before the table, I grated as much carrot as I needed on to the newspaper, then added to it an equal amount of mocking-bird food, mixed it thoroughly with the knife, then laid it away in the paper for use. I then produced from the cupboard a dish-pan, which I filled with scalding suds, and placed on the table with dish-mop and towels; then a pitcher of fresh water and two or three tin quart boxes of seed, which I put on a smaller table one side.

Then I was ready to begin my work of clearing up. From all the cages I took the dishes — often there were twenty — emptied the sour or dry mocking-bird food, blew off the shells, and emptied the seed-cups, dropping every one into the hot suds, from which they emerged clean and smoking, and were wiped and set on the other table, all of one kind together. While they were cooling, ready to receive the food, I took out every perch that was soiled, scraped it and washed it in the suds, using a brush for the purpose. In the winter I piled them on the register to dry; when I had no fire, I stood them against the window-pane in the sun.

By this time my dishes were cool, and I filled each one with fresh water, or the prepared food, or replenished the seed, according to the need.

Then I began with the seed-eaters, who are neater than the soft-food birds, and cleaned every tray thus: emptying the gravel on to a folded newspaper, I washed the tray in the hot suds (using the mop), wiped it, and dried it over the register; then, using a small sieve I sifted out all the dirt and shells, and returned the gravel to the tray, adding a shake or two from the box of fresh gravel. About once a fortnight I threw this all out, and began again with fresh gravel. When one tray was in order I replaced it, adding the food and water dishes that belonged to it, and then proceeded to the next.

So I went through the room, leaving every

bird-cage in perfect order, with food for the day. Then I carried away my dish-washing tools, hung up my towels, put away my food boxes and cans, and prepared the table for bathing.

When everything was ready (as described in Chapter VII.) I made sure that all the windows were right, blinds put up, lace curtains down —if a green bird was to come out—and the room doors latched. Then I opened every cage door, put in the door perches, and took my seat at my desk to rest and enjoy the bathing. In a moment the birds began to come out; some rushed at once to the bathing-table and began to splash, some flew around the room, to try their wings, and others went to the sunny windows; but the knowing ones came to my desk to ask for meal-worms, or soaked currants, or raw beef, whichever dainty they happened to prefer. I gave out the tidbits, tossing a wriggling worm to the floor, where it was instantly seized, or holding it gingerly at the end of my long tweezers for a bolder bird to snatch. The currants I held in my fingers generally, and one after another they would come shyly up and help themselves.

After all had bathed, and pluming and dressing of feathers were going on everywhere, I brought out my special treats. In summer there were huckleberries for the clarine; pears for the orchard oriole; sorrel, or chickweed, or plantain for the seed-eaters. In winter, slices of apple and soaked currants for all. These I placed in the cages. The bird would go in and taste, and make sure that he was supplied, and then come out and play about, try all the perches, and amuse himself in many ways, while I sat on the farther side of the room, note-book in hand, and took notes of all the funny and serious things that went on among them. I remained motionless and perfectly silent, wishing not to have them notice me, and they often did seem to forget my presence entirely.

When I started my bird colony, I used to leave the doors open till late afternoon. But I found a good deal of trouble in getting the birds back, because before dark (on a winter day as early as four o'clock) each bird settled himself somewhere — it might be in and it might be out of the cage—and appeared bewildered if forced to move. As I was obliged to open the windows at night and let the room get cool, it was necessary to protect them, and I could not do it unless they were at home. So I occasionally had to catch one in my hand and return him to his cage, which I did not like any better than he did.

On closer study of my small tenants, I found that after noon they did not move about much, but sat quietly and sang; so day after day I shut them up earlier and earlier, till at last I found they were just as happy and satisfied to have the door closed at noon as later. That came to be the rule, therefore; every door was fastened before two o'clock, and the birds almost invariably spent the whole afternoon singing.

To close the doors without startling and without approaching them (which made some timid ones dash out), I thought out a plan by which I could shut every one without leaving my seat. I fastened, by a loop easily removed, a fine strong twine to each door, and by means of staples or "double tacks" driven into window-casings below the window, I carried each line through its own set of staples around to my desk. Down the side of the desk was a row of small nails, and each line (looped at the end) was just long enough, when the door it held was wide open, to let its loop slip over its own particular nail.

When I opened the doors in the morning, every string was drawn taut, and each loop over its nail. As closing-up time drew near, I sat at my desk with an eye to the birds, and when one went home I slipped his loop off the nail, let the door gently close, and then dropped the string. So I went on till all were shut up.

To shut the door quickly and quietly I had several devices — doors that moved with a spring were simply held straight back, and it needed only to slacken the string to close them; doors that slid up, and were not heavy enough to fall of their own weight, were weighted with strips of lead fastened across the bottom; then, on loosening the string that held it up, the weight drew it to place. For a door that closed from the side with a spring, I passed the string from the upper corner of the door forward through the wires at the place where that corner would be when shut, and then I had to draw tight in order to shut.

9

When all were in I went quietly around and removed door perches and unhooked the strings from the cage doors, letting the latter hang from their staples. Then I hooked the loops at the other end of the strings all back in their places at my desk. Thus to fasten them open in the morning, I simply gathered up the ends next the cages, and slipped each into its place on the door. I have described this in detail, as I have everything else about my arrangements, because I have been so often begged to tell exactly how I managed my bird-room.

The birds in, I left them to their own devices till bedtime, when I had more work to make them comfortable for the night. If it were warm weather, and there were any mosquitoes about, I wrapped every cage in mosquito-netting, which I kept of appropriate size. In cold weather each cage was carefully protected with a woollen cover, usually some old shawl, a thin blanket, or a worn piano cover.

It will readily be seen from this true account of my daily work—which, moreover, does not half tell the story—that keeping birds healthy and happy in a room is by no means child's play. It requires genuine love for the birds, and willingness to give up nearly all one's time to them. I earnestly hope that no one will attempt it who cannot heartily give both.

XIII

THE AVIARY

IF one has not room, or for any reason prefers not to give the time and trouble necessary to maintain what I have called a bird-room, he or she may find much enjoyment with an aviary. The distinction I make between the two is this: in the former, human beings may also live, with almost no inconvenience, since the homes of the birds are in cages, even though these may stand open most of the time, while an aviary is an apartment entirely given up to birds without cages.

The largest aviary I have seen was tenanted by two hundred canaries, and it gave great delight to every one who visited it, in spite of the fact that a canary shows less intelligence than most of our native birds. Being a regular cage product, he appears, like a slave born of a race of slaves, to lack some of the wide-awake acuteness of birds born in freedom.

Many of our familiar birds, and, I believe, most of the smaller foreign birds brought to our country, will live peaceably together under certain conditions. Indeed, such a "happy family" arrangement is frequently seen in the windows of our bird dealers, where bluebirds and sparrows, orioles and cedar-birds, sometimes many others, are to be seen in one big show cage. In the small menageries common in our city parks, also, may often be seen a large cage with a dozen or more different sorts of birds living together in peace.

The "conditions" spoken of as necessary to success are two. The first is abundance of room. Any individual, be he bird, beast, or even human, will be made irritable by constant companionship. Every one, even a little bird, needs opportunity occasionally to get away from his fellows.

An ample bay-window, separated from the room by coarse wire gauze, or, better still, a small apartment exclusively their own, may be made the happy home of half a dozen birds. If a cage is used for an aviary it must be very large indeed, or only a few birds kept in it, unless they be the tiny African finches, who do not seem to mind living in a crowd.

The second condition of contentment is plenty of accommodations, such as numerous seed and water cups, several bathing-dishes, and every delicacy, such as fruit or green food, duplicated more than once, so that one or two selfish fellows may not be able to monopolize. I have seen a bird when he could eat no more, yet was still unwilling to share his food with a cage mate, actually seat himself in the dish, and remain there as long as he could stand it to keep quiet. I do not say there must be a set for every bird, but there should be at least one for every two birds.

Ample accommodations, too, mean plenty of perches, with several having as nearly as possible the same attractiveness, for sleeping perches. Almost all small cage birds want to sleep on the very top round, and if the highest is only one, and perhaps a small one at that, one strong and selfish bird can keep it for his own use, and make the rest unhappy; while if there are half a dozen equally desirable, he may drive them off his, but they can find others as satisfactory. A row of sleeping birds, all puffed out into fluffy balls, with feet hidden, and heads tucked snugly out of sight under their shoulder feathers, blue and yellow and brown and red, side by side, is a lovely sight.

Everything, indeed, that is placed in an aviary must be several times duplicated to avoid jealousy and contention. For example, a bathing-dish to every three or four birds is indispensable, unless the one provided is so wide and shallow that half a dozen may use it at once. The birds are sure to wish to bathe all at the same time, and scarcity of accommodation makes trouble at once. Green food—apple, sorrel, or lettuce—should be put in several separate places, so that no one or two can appropriate the whole.

With all these precautions, a close watch must be kept to see that no one tyrannizes over another, for our little brothers of the air are surprisingly human in their characteristics. Among them will be found the glutton, the bully, and the tyrant, as well as the gentle, the timid, and the unassuming, to be their victims. I have had a bird starved to death by the selfishness of a cage mate, and never suspected it, closely as I study my birds.

The floor of an aviary must be thickly spread with fine gravel or sand, which should be brushed out and changed as often as every fortnight, and the floor washed. The lady who had a room given up to birds, which I have already referred to, bought her gravel or coarse sand by the barrel, as well as her bird-seed.

Cleanliness and frequent washing of dishes and scalding of perches are just as important in an aviary as in a bird-room; and since the birds cannot be covered up individually, the room must be kept at a nearly even temperature.

If a bird is ill he must be instantly removed from the rest, and kept in a cage till well, both that he may have quiet, medicine, and proper food, and that he may not infect the rest, as in some disorders he would by drinking from the common cups. If the stock is all of one kind, and it is desired that they shall nest, proper places must be prepared; little baskets, such as come for cage nesting, may be fastened up in quiet nooks, and material suitable for lining placed within reach.

When the young are able to be fed, food proper for them must be kept ready. Direc-

tions for preparing food for sitting birds and
their young will be found in books devoted to
raising canaries; I have had no experience of
that kind.

The bird family to which I have alluded
more than once was kept for a good many
years—perhaps is to this day—in a room in
the upper story of a house in Brooklyn. The
mistress of it had at the time I knew it, several years ago, two hundred canaries, all raised
from two or three pairs; and because she had
not room for more she was obliged to discour-
age their nesting. At one time when I went to
see them a persistent little bird had "stolen
her nest," as poultry-raisers say. She collected
enough stuff for an apology for a nest, placed
it on the door-sill, and there the brave little
creature was brooding her eggs where every
one who entered had to step over her. It was
a touching sight, and the mistress could not
bring herself to break up the nest so confiding-
ly placed.

With all these busy, happy canaries—and I
never saw a livelier colony—a solitary bluebird dwelt in peace and contentment. He had
been brought to her injured in some way, and

as an experiment she put him into the bird-room. At first the little yellow fellows were in awe of one so big; but finding him a well-disposed personage, they accepted him as a room-mate, and paid no further attention to him. Outside the walls of this happy bird home lived another bird, whom the mistress did not dare trust within—a mocking-bird. Constant entertainment was furnished him by his stirring little neighbors. He was as interested in their ways and doings as any child in a circus. He often stood for an hour at a time with attention fixed upon them, following their movements with his eyes, and uttering his sentiments now and then in a low cluck.

It has been said that the mocking-bird cannot imitate the canary song, but this bird sang the canary aria frequently, louder and better than the canaries themselves. It was curious to note the effect of his performance on the small birds. When he began every note ceased; every little yellow head turned to see who it was that so outdid them. They were not discouraged, however; they were too happy, and the music was too infectious to resist.

In a few moments they joined in, in chorus, and then the house fairly rang with canary songs.

A celebrated aviary was maintained by an English resident in China, and described nearly sixty years ago by Mr. Bennett, the naturalist. This aviary was twenty feet wide and forty long, and nearly as many feet in height made of what he calls wire lattice. In this bird-house were trees and shrubs, with nesting-baskets for such of the tenants as wished to use them. A large supply of water for all, and rock-work for birds who liked it, were provided. Not only every need, but every wish of the birds—so far as known—was gratified. There were even cages to use as places of solitary confinement for belligerent or selfish birds, who, if they refused to learn wisdom under this treatment, were finally cast out of the bird paradise, and forced to take care of themselves.

An aviary is perhaps not so much care as a bird-room, and it is in some ways more satisfactory; that is, if it is large enough to give play to the individuality of birds, like those I have mentioned. If it is so small as to be a mere house, where the birds jostle and irritate each other, it is of no particular interest.

The directions I have given for perches, dishes, and food in a bird-room will apply equally to an aviary.

XIV

THE DOG AS A PET

THE custom, old as the human race, of taking beasts and birds into the house as companions and friends of the family, is one of great interest. Not only do the creatures thus placed under foreign and unnatural conditions afford interesting subjects of study, but they are useful in many ways, as protectors of our property, guardians of our children, and safety-valves for unplaced affections. And besides these most obvious uses, when properly appreciated and enjoyed, they offer unequalled opportunity for lessons to our children in humanity, justice, and unselfishness. Moreover, they furnish an ever-fresh source of happiness to those who love them ; happiness, too, without alloy, since no conduct of theirs, however base, can hurt us like the unkind words or deeds of a human friend.

Of all the pets we gather about us, the dog

usually comes the nearest to being absolutely
one of the family. Not that he has greater intelligence than the cat, or some of the birds;
but he identifies himself more completely with
his human friends, and is much more demonstrative than others. Long years of dependence and companionship have attached him to
our race, and made him almost incapable of
doing without us. A lost dog is one of the
most hopeless and wretched creatures in existence, and it is really pitiful to see his attempts to attach himself to somebody. He will,
figuratively speaking, go down on his knees in
the dust to any one who does not utterly re-
pulse him, and beg in the most touching way
to be adopted.

Not only does the dog become as one of the
family, but in many cases he gets to be the
autocrat of the household, his convenience de-
ciding all questions of family policy, and his
tastes and his notions consulted before those
of any human member. Often, indeed, he becomes to every one excepting his doting mistress an intolerable nuisance.

The dog of fashion is an expensive luxury
in our day. He requires almost as many be-

longings as his mistress—elegant upholstered apartments, satin and velvet cushions, and a bed as good as the house affords; travelling-satchels and napping-baskets, various garments, table service and toilet articles, playthings, ribbons, costly harness, and valuable jewelry set with gems. There is hardly an end to his possessions. Besides this, he often has a maid specially devoted to his service, and he gives luncheon parties. When ill, he is attended by the family physician, if the latter is either very humane or afraid of losing patronage; and when he dies he is buried in a costly casket, and commemorated by a marble monument, though sometimes he is scientifically "preserved," placed in a jewelled receptacle too valuable to be buried, and kept on exhibition in the home his death has made desolate. A dog thus treated has almost ceased to be a dog. He is a product of fashion, and seems hardly to belong to the race of "doggy" dogs, whom we all love and like to have about us.

So intimate for generations has been the dog's relation with the human race that he is truly becoming almost painfully like us. Not only does he possess most of our virtues, but our vices, alas! are reflected in him as in a mirror; vanity, self-consciousness, love of notoriety, thirst for excitement and curiosity, all show themselves full-blown in the pet of the fireside.

This being the case, introducing one of these animals into the house is almost like adding another member to the family, and it should be done intelligently. Not only should one be clear as to his purpose in wanting a pet, but he should study the qualities of the various breeds, and decide with deliberation which will best meet the demand.

Let him ask himself, first, for what he desires a dog. Is it for protection, as a playmate for children, as an ornament to the house, as a companion for himself, or for purposes of general utility? Suppose the need is for protection; in the country an animal is required large enough and savage enough to attack a tramp or a thief, and hold him; while for the same use in the city, a small one who barks an alarm is equally efficient. If what is desired is a playmate for children, there is a like difference in choice. The country child,

THE FAMILY PET

wandering about the roads and fields, needs a dog of a size and disposition to protect him, and if near the water, to rescue him when he falls in, as he is tolerably certain to do; but the duties of the city child's dog are more strictly those of a playfellow, to entertain and amuse by his gambols.

If a house ornament is the object sought, a St. Bernard or Great Dane that will fitly adorn a large place by his dimensions will unpleasantly dwarf any ordinary town residence. The beautiful little spaniels, the so-called "toy dogs," more properly decorate a city parlor.

If the demand is for a companion, intellect and affection are the things to seek, and the size does not so much matter, though a very large dog can rarely have in city homes room and exercise enough for his health. For an all-around useful animal, one of the medium-sized dogs, such as a spaniel or collie, combines the most desirable qualities.

Another point to consider is the harmony of the dog with his surroundings, for it would be no less inappropriate to place one of the dainty, sensitive, luxury-loving toy dogs in a busy, bustling country household, than to keep a Great Dane or a St. Bernard in an elegant apartment, or a narrow brick-on-end-shaped city house.

It should be well understood in the beginning that a pet is a great deal of trouble, and no one should assume the care unless he is willing to bear the burden. To surround ourselves with these helpless dependants, and then neglect to provide for their comfort and happiness, is not merely cruel, it is really a crime. As already said, taking a dog into the family is like adopting a child, and one is just as responsible for neglect of duty towards one as towards the other.

When one really goes out to select and buy a dog, especially if he has no preferences, it is important that he should educate himself— and by himself, of course, I also mean herself. This is best done, perhaps, by "reading up" on the different varieties, and then visiting some good kennels, or, if possible, a dog show, for the looks and appearance of an animal have much to do with our liking for him.

Should we select his variety and then buy a puppy? That depends; puppies are charming; no young creature is more so, for though they lack the perfect grace, the bewitching playfulness, the altogether irresistible charms of the kitten, they have yet a winning innocence of mien and a delightful clumsiness of bearing that are almost equally attractive. But puppies have another side, alas! It is true that the dog in his babyhood is funny, but he is also mischievous. It is certainly comical to see him frolic with an old shoe, a door-mat, or some discarded garment; but when he snatches clothes from the line, worries one's best boots, or drags off a valuable table-cover in his pranks, it ceases to be amusing, and he will do one as readily as the other.

It is gratifying to possess a canine follower that one has brought up and trained, but the process requires patience, gentleness, and long-suffering; in fact, the ordinary mortal needs special training in these virtues himself to fit him for the task. Besides the pains required, there is the risk. Baby dogs are almost as prone to disease as baby humans. They may not, to be sure, suffer from croup or scarlet-fever, but they have their own infant disorders, quite as apt to be fatal.

Because of this uncertainty of life, a young

puppy of almost any breed may be bought at a low price. Usually ten or fifteen dollars will procure a promising specimen of a kind that, when safely past his first year, will bring from seventy-five dollars to twenty-five thousand dollars, at which price some valuable animals are held.

In making choice, one hint may be useful. After seeing that all the " points " which show good blood are present, the buyer should look carefully on the body behind the fore-legs, and also behind the ears, for indications of irritation, and promptly reject the most promising dog who shows any such sign. Shaking the head is also an evidence of disease which should not be unheeded.

> " For ways that are dark,
> And tricks that are [not always] vain,"

the dog-dealer has a reputation second only to that of the horse-dealer. One needs to go armed with accurate knowledge, and even then a thoroughly informed friend, or a responsible agent, is safer. It would undoubtedly be better to buy at the kennels, of which New York has several readily accessible, than to take one's pet at second-hand.

XV

THE BIG DOGS

IN this book the dog will be considered merely in his relation to the family, and his availability for the companionship of women and children. I shall give brief descriptions of the different breeds ordinarily kept in the household, with the principal " points " that testify to purity of the blood, characteristics, and qualifications of each for life in the home, and, lastly, hints as to care in health and disease.

The Great Dane is entitled to the palm for size, the tallest reaching the enormous height of thirty-four inches, and exceeding by about half an inch the utmost record of his rival, the great St. Bernard. He does not, however, show the clumsiness that might be expected from his measurement, for he is well built. He has a fine head, with clear, expressive eyes, a tail held level with the back, and

curving a little upward at the tip. The perfect Dane is not too heavy, and though he will
generally fall below the figures given as the
maximum, he should not lack more than four
or five inches of that height, and should bring
the scales down to between one hundred and
twenty and one hundred and twenty - five
pounds. Bowed fore-legs are to be avoided,
and spreading toes are a decided blemish.
The coat of this dog should be glossy, and if
it is spotted with black on a white ground,
its wearer is entitled to the first rank and the
highest value. Blue spots on a very light
ground are admissible, however, as are also
tigerlike stripes and a plain color.

As to his fitness for domestication, opinions
differ. No one questions his courage as a
protector of property; to dispose of a tramp
or a burglar is mere play to him. But while
admirers assert that he is easily controlled
and gentle with children, many persons declare, on the contrary, that he is always a dangerous inmate of the household, being, when
roused, savage towards friend as well as foe.
Of course, dogs of the same family differ in
temperament, and unquestionably an entirely

amiable Great Dane is not an impossibility, though he may be rare. It is, or has been, the custom to cut the ears of this animal, but a sentiment in favor of nature's work is growing among the more intelligent dog-raisers.

Practically equal in size to this canine giant, and a much more beautiful animal, is the great St. Bernard, whose value when perfect is far up in the tens of thousands. His well-known history gives him a reputation for nobility of character which is borne out by facts, and no dog of his size is his equal in gentleness, sagacity, and attachment to his friends. As a protector he is vigilant and faithful, and at the same time he possesses more sense and discretion than most of his kind. Children seem to be his special care, and he cannot be excelled as a country companion for them.

There are two kinds of St. Bernards—the rough and the smooth coated. The former is more beautiful, but is also much more care. His slightly wavy coat needs so much attention to be kept in proper condition that he actually should have a servant for his own use. In color he should be red and white in varying combinations, with patches of dark brindle color. A white breast is indispensable, white also around the nose, at the end of the tail, and if he has a bit on the nape of the neck, and a blaze, so much the better. Should he happen to be without white, he is nobody in the St. Bernard family. Any other colors than those mentioned are undesirable.

The third of the big dogs is the mastiff, of soft fawn-color, with black ears and muzzle, and short, smooth coat. About no dog do opinions differ more widely than about this one—his friends declaring him a pattern of virtue, while his enemies are just as positive that he is a monster of vice, some going so far as to call him a man-eater. There is no doubt that he will faithfully protect his master's property, and all agree that when once roused he is furious, and no man or beast is safe from his rage. Kindly cared for, he is said to be peaceable and gentle with children ; but if he considers himself unjustly treated, he will fly at his best-loved friend. However valuable he may be as a protector in a country-place, he is certainly unfitted for the city, where it is difficult to give him enough exercise to keep him in health.

To keep any one of these large dogs happy, and consequently healthy, he should have a house of his own; and still better, if possible, some one especially to care for him. He needs a great amount of exercise, and a chain or a muzzle is exceedingly distasteful to him.

It is agreeable, after considering these monsters of the race, to speak of one who is wholly delightful — the Newfoundland. Intelligent and courageous, yet not savage or ugly, always kind to children, and especially valuable as a water-dog, being perfectly fearless and a remarkable swimmer. He should be jet black, with a glossy coat, coarse in texture, rather close and somewhat wavy, but not at all curly. A white breast and toes do not detract from his value; but a tail with a kink in it, or curling over the back, is entirely inadmissible.

The coach-dog, or Dalmatian, is much admired for his striking markings, and has had his turn at being the fashion. He is white, with black or liver-colored spots scattered all over him, from ears to tip of tail. These spots should be round, and not larger than a half-dollar, preferably black. A black face or black ears detract greatly from his value. It is pleasing to note that it is not now the fashion to clip this dog's ears. The predominant trait in the coach-dog seems to be his fondness for horses; indeed, those who do not like him say he is fit for nothing but to be the companion of a stableman, certainly not at all suitable for a house pet. His proper place with a carriage is running under the fore axle.

The bull-dog is considered beautiful in exact proportion to his ugliness. The more his nose turns up, and the greater number of ugly wrinkles he can show, the higher is his value. Indeed, it is intended that he should be ugly in temper, corresponding with his looks, and he is naturally a blood-thirsty beast. Yet, on the other hand, he is said to be affectionate and gentle to children, unless his temper is soured by being regarded as only a protector, and kept chained — treatment that turns the most gentle into a savage. He is suitable only for the country.

The big hounds can hardly be said to come under the head of house-dogs, and they are entirely out of place in the city. The English greyhound is very attractive in the country, where there is plenty of room, for exercise is indispensable to him. He is an aristocratic personage, both dainty and dignified, and, in fact, he is said to possess almost human characteristics. His coat should be short, neither woolly nor too fine. He should be treated like a reasonable being, for he is extremely sensitive to injustice and cruelty.

The setters are, in the opinion of many dog-lovers, the most beautiful and noble of their kind. In considering the varieties of a race noted for its subserviency to man, it is truly refreshing to come upon one with a reputation for independence of character. When to that quality is added strong individuality, unusual intelligence, and a beautiful coat of long red hair, the attractiveness of the red Irish setter is explained. In color he is either a rich mahogany red, of which there are two shades, or a golden chestnut, without black. White may be allowed on chest and toes, a little on the forehead, or a narrow stripe on the face, but nowhere else. His ears should be set on low, and hang close to the head.

The way a dog carries his tail is of the greatest importance in the eye of the fancier; the Newfoundland may let his hang, and the pug may curl his over his back, but should an Irish setter follow the fashion of either, he would be condemned without mercy. He must carry his caudal appendage perfectly straight, and on a level with his spine. This beautiful beast seems really to embody all the canine virtues—faithfulness, intelligence, gentleness with children, watchfulness, and discrimination, the last exceedingly desirable.

The Gordon and the English setters are also favorite house-dogs, and noted for about the same qualities. All are as ornamental as they are useful.

Pointers have the reputation of being not so good-tempered as setters, and therefore not so safe in families. Both require a great deal of exercise and a judicious restriction in diet, and both setters and pointers seem better fitted for an active out-door life than for the parlor.

The Eskimo dog and the spitz are so unsuited to this climate and suffer so much from heat that it is a cruelty to keep them. The latter, moreover, has the reputation, whether justly or not, of being apt to go mad.

XVI

THE MIDDLE-SIZED DOGS

IT is impossible to draw exact lines of division in a race which ranges from four inches to thirty-four in height, with representatives at every inch between. The large ones shade into the middle-sized ones so gradually that the collie, for example, might with equal propriety end the list of the one or begin that of the other. I place him among the middle-sized because these intermediates between the giants and the toys are the most desirable for home dogs, in either city or country, and his qualities entitle him to take the lead.

The collie is a real dog, such as we love and remember from childhood, with characteristics that make him invaluable in the family life. Intelligent above most of his race, sagacious, gentle, affectionate; adapting himself perfectly to the family ways, requiring little care in winter or summer, safe in all places and on all occasions, with no troublesome inclination to worry cats or other animals, he is really the ideal dog for a household. To be fashionable he should be black with white points, but he is one of the few with whom varieties in color may be indulged in without total loss of caste. He may wear tan with his black instead of white, if fate so decrees. His tail should be long, carried low, and turned upward at the end; his coat straight, hard, and rather stiff, with an under coat thick and furry. The "ruff," which is one of his beauties, should be very full, but he must not, if he wishes to be perfect, show much "feather" on the legs—none at all on the hinder pair.

He should have access to water, or, if in the city, be washed once a week in summer. One of the pleasantest recollections of a summer in the Berkshire Hills is of the family collie cooling himself by lying flat in the bed of a lively mountain brook till his thick coat was soaked through.

A little anecdote of a collie will illustrate the character of the family better than anything I could say. The story is vouched for as true, and the incident occurred nearly one hundred and fifty years ago, in the early days of our nation—during the French and Indian war, in fact.

The dog was a great pet in the family of a colonial soldier, and was particularly noted for his antipathy to Indians, whom he delighted to track. On one campaign against the French the dog insisted on accompanying his master, although his feet were in a terrible condition from having been frozen the preceding winter. During the fight which ended in the famous Braddock defeat, the collie was beside his beloved master; but when it was over they had become separated, and the soldier, concluding his pet had been killed, went home without him. Some weeks later, however, the dog appeared in his old home, separated from the battle-field by many miles and thick forests. He was tired and worn, but over his sore feet were fastened neat moccasins, showing that he had been among Indians who had been kind to him. Moreover, he soon showed that he had changed his mind about his former foe, for neither bribes nor threats could ever again induce him to track an Indian. His generous nature could not forget a kindness, even to please those he loved enough to seek under so great difficulties.

While the collie is good in doors and out, as a parlor pet or a general care-taker on a farm, the poodle is fit only for the house. One can hardly imagine one of these shaven and shorn artificial products of fashion living out-of-doors with other dogs. As regards the beauty of the poodle, there is room for a wide difference of opinion. One who thinks that Nature knows how to form and decorate her dogs will not admire the elaborate shaving in patterns, after diagrams laid down in a book, the "bracelets" standing out like a stiff clothes-brush, the broomlike feet, the mustachios, and other grotesque ornaments of the fashionable poodle. Happily he's a sunny-tempered fellow, and submits to the caprices of fashion with a better grace than many dogs would. He is one of the most intelligent of the race, the chosen trick dog, and more ready to learn than any other. He is also a remarkable swimmer and keen of scent, but full of mischief and pranks.

Three kinds of poodles are familiar to us in

America—the German, the French, and the barbet. The first named is the largest, and usually solid black or white, though he sometimes has a white star on the breast, or a white toe or two. His coat is long, coarse, and almost wiry, with a strong tendency to work itself into strings—or " cords," as technically called—not bigger than a large twine. These cords should be all over the body except about the face, and the longer the better. To leave no part of his body untouched, this victim of man's desire to improve upon nature has part of his tail cut off.

The French poodle differs in some respects from his German brother. He is a little smaller, and his thick and woolly coat tends to curl rather than to cord. The barbet is the dwarf of the family, being not more than eight or ten inches high, covered with snow-white ringlets. He is a bright, active little fellow, fond of fun, and quick to learn tricks. The barbet is said not to be so amiable as could be desired ; in fact, apt to be somewhat snappish.

All poodles require much care to keep their peculiar coats in order. They cannot be combed, and they must not be scratched. If the owner of a handsome curled or corded coat is not content to suffer in order to be beautiful, if he will scratch, he must be clad in mittens, and if his ear is the point of attack, a cap must be added to make certain that he does not injure the hair. It is only common humanity that the greatest care should be taken to keep him free from fleas, so that he will not wish to scratch.

The dachshund and the beagle, two small hounds, may be kept in the city, but it is imperative that they have plenty of exercise. The former has one quality that makes him troublesome in town — a ruling passion for fight. Walking the streets with his mistress, he will pick a quarrel with every dog he meets, from a mastiff to a toy terrier. Moreover, he is a dog of ideas and independence; he will mind if the command meets his approval, not otherwise. He is said also to be exceedingly destructive to garments and furs, which he tears to pieces. He is not a beauty, having a long body and very short bandy-legs; but he is valuable, almost priceless, say his admirers.

If one race was especially formed for the city house-dog, it could not meet the demand better than the spaniels. All of them are vivacious, full of amusing tricks, affectionate, good watch-dogs, and delightful playmates. Even the water-spaniel will flourish and be happy in a city house if he is taken to the water now and then.

For a city house the cocker spaniel has perhaps the greatest number of friends. He has all the virtues of his race—intelligence, fidelity, good temper, and attachment to people; he is an excellent playfellow for children, and the best of watch-dogs. Moreover, he is less noisy than many of his kind, and suffers less from confinement in a house; for while he is very lively and perfectly happy out-of-doors, he also enjoys the comfort of lying about the house. He is especially interested in the panorama of life in the streets, which he will watch from a window with great eagerness.

This little fellow seems more nearly human than most dogs, being very self-respecting, and painfully sensitive to ridicule or harshness. He should be treated with justice and dignity, and never scolded or struck. In addition to all this, he is one of the handsomest of our four-footed pets, whether he is liver-colored, with or without white, or white and black. His weight should be about twelve pounds, his legs not too long, but well " feathered," and it is the fashion to cut his tail. He has a beautiful head, and bright, intelligent eyes. No one who selects a cocker spaniel for a pet will be apt to regret it.

THE BEGGING SPANIEL

XVII

THE SMALL DOGS

THERE seems to be no use in trying to supersede the pug in the affections of the family. New dogs are brought out, and old ones pushed to the front; Europe is scoured for novelties, and Asia is laid under contribution; still the little black nose of puggy is seen everywhere, still his soft satin skin nestles on velvet cushions, and his absurd little tail curls tighter than ever in the proud consciousness that he is yet, as he has been for so long, the favorite dog for the city home.

Nor is it any wonder, for the pug seems to combine in his own substantial little body the greater share of the dog virtues—good temper, which makes him patiently endure the rough fondling of the nursery; lively disposition, which renders him a cheerful companion; playfulness, that places him first in the affections of the children; and watchful care of the household, that proves him a valuable guardian. He is, moreover free from the odor that is almost inseparable from his race, and exceedingly offensive to ours, and for personal neatness he is not to be surpassed. What more could we ask in a house-dog? It is true that he is not so intelligent as some others — the cocker spaniel, for instance — but he is no fool for all that. He is a born aristocrat, declining to associate with the outcast dogs of the street, and he bears himself with a dignity that in one of his size is very amusing. One cannot help becoming attached to the little beastie.

The pug, as we generally see him on the street or in the home of abundance, is too fat. His graceful proportions are lost, his liveliness is lessened, and he reminds one too strongly of his grosser relative, the bull-dog. The weight of puggy should never be allowed to reach twenty pounds — twelve is better. His markings should be very pronounced and very black, his nose blunt, square, and like satin; his ears and the back line, the moles, and the thumb-marks that distinguish him, of the most ebony hue. Then if the wrinkles that proclaim not age but blood are strong and deep, his color a delicate fawn, the top of his head square, and his ears drooping towards the front, he may be set down as perfection, and of the bluest blood of the pug race.

The pug appreciates his position as prime favorite, and understands what that position demands. He accepts the manners and customs of civilization, resists not the bath, submits cheerfully to tooth-brush and perfumery; rebels not at bangles, blankets, and silver bands on the neck, and will endure the most enormous of bows without a murmur. He is willingly carried in a dog-satchel, or by a handle fastened to his harness, and he regards satin cushions, elegant dog-baskets, and other luxuries as his right. Long may he reign in the world of pets!

A dog who was intended to oust puggy from his place of honor in the household, but who has not as yet succeeded in doing it, is the schipperke, or Belgian "spitz," who is said to be related to the spitz or Pomeranian that we are familiar with; he certainly resembles him. The perfect schipperke (or "chipperke," as he is sometimes called) is solid black, with a sharp nose, and small ears rather close together. His eyes are small and brown, and his feet round, with black toe-nails. His tail—alas, he has none! If Nature endows him with one (which she does not, as a usual thing), it is at once cut off, as entirely out of place in a schipperke.

This dog has many virtues. He is knowing and full of pranks, enjoys learning tricks, which cannot be said of many of his kind. He is lively, graceful, and comely, as well as hardy, and he is naturally very neat. No dog is more alert and interested in affairs around him, and none more affectionate to his friends. The Belgian spitz should weigh somewhat less than a dozen pounds, and be dressed in rather coarse hair an inch long and very thick on the body, but longer about the neck, where it literally stands up in excitement. It is also somewhat longer down the spine, and it hangs in a mass to hide his tailless condition. He is in fashion at the present moment, and a perfect schipperke is rare.

Well known, though no longer on the top wave of fashion, are the terriers, both smooth and rough. None the less, however, are they desirable in the family. The black-and-tan, a bundle of frolic and liveliness, is perhaps the most familiar. He now comes within the reach of many who are not able to indulge in the latest canine fancy, and is just as valuable in the household as when he was rare and costly. He is clean, and requires little care, because of his short coat. He does not disfigure the cushions with white hairs, as does the fox-terrier, and a burglar need be a master indeed who could enter a house which he guards. The black-and-tan will live and be happy under conditions that many dogs could not endure, in doors or out, cuddled, blanketed, and ribboned, or left to look out for himself, and he does not lose his temper or mope in either case. "Rats" is the magic word that will rouse every fibre of his being, and to destroy them in his ruling passion.

This dog has become so common that mongrels are every day seen, and one who desires a pure-blooded animal should look carefully to his points. His weight should not be over twenty pounds, and considerably less is better; his coat shining, but not soft, and his tail should not curl. In color he must be glossy black, with sharply defined markings of tan, and no white. Of the tan-color should be a spot over each eye and on both cheeks, the lips and underjaw, and inside of the legs. Black lines should run up through the tan on every toe, and the hue of the tan should border on red.

Not so desirable as this charming house-dog is his relative, the bull-terrier. He has his good qualities, of course. As a guardian he is unsurpassed, and for courage and persistence no dog is more distinguished. But, on the other hand, fighting is his dearest delight; no dog and no strange man can expect mercy at his hands. It is said that he can be taught to be kind to children, but it is somewhat risky to depend upon a cultivated virtue, and it is safer to select some other breed for a house pet.

A great favorite with many people is the fox-terrier, with his short, easily-kept-clean coat, and his lively temperament. He has many doggish virtues — attachment to his friends, amusing ways, fondness for a house life, and willingness to be petted, and he is cleanly and inoffensive as regards odor. The greatest drawback to his desirableness as a companion for the house is his almost incurable habit of barking on all and every occasion. The entrance of a friend and the approach of a possible enemy alike arouse his sharp, deafening barks, and nothing short of absolute beheading will stop him. For any one with "nerves," therefore, the fox-terrier cannot be recommended as a house pet, though for an out-of-doors dog he has many admirable qualities.

The very name terrier suggests the deadly enemy of the rat. The rough-coated of the race are no less devoted to that particular form of "sport" than the smooth. First, and perhaps best known, is the Irish, with rich brown coat of rather harsh texture, and eyes not quite so entirely veiled with hair as his fellow rough-coats; a good watcher, and friendly with the little folk. Next, the Scotch, resembling his brother of the Emerald Isle in disposition and dress, but of lighter hue, not much deeper than cream-color; and, lastly, the Dandie Dinmont, clothed in hair that may be called "a fine mix," and possessing the good qualities of his Irish and Scotch brethren.

There is one danger in introducing a small dog into the house that should not be overlooked, for it affects the character of our children. The submission of a creature who notoriously will "kiss the hand that beats him" has not a good influence on our boys. The control of a dog tends strongly to develop in his young master inhumanity, disrespect for the rights of others, and an overwhelming self-conceit. The large dog will make himself respected, the smaller one will not, and unless parents are very watchful to counteract the evil effects of unlimited authority, they will find their boy growing rapidly in brutality and conceit, and by so much failing of the nobility of character they desire to cultivate in him. A pet that will assert its own rights, and enforce respect by teeth or claws, is therefore a better aid in the development of character than the all-enduring and all-forgiving small dog.

XVIII

THE "TOYS"

THE old-fashioned name for the tiny dogs we call toys, "lapdogs," quaintly indicates where to draw this line between our household animals. They are dogs small enough to be held in the lap, and they are emphatically pets for the parlor, requiring the care of my lady herself, or of her deputy, a well-trained maid.

Let us begin with the Skye, the droll little bundle of hair who has hardly enough leg to get about on — so short, indeed, that his long hair almost sweeps the ground as he waddles about. His deficiency in height is amply atoned for by his length, for he comes perilously near to resembling the weasel tribe, being at least three times as long as he is high. Nine or ten inches tall and twenty-five or thirty inches long is his approved measurement, and the weight considered proper for these inches is from sixteen to seventeen pounds.

The Skye-terrier comes in two varieties. One of them rejoices in pretty, long, hanging ears, and a tail which droops gracefully to correspond; the other matches his pert little standing ears with a caudal appendage that scorns to droop in the least. Both of the little beasties have long coarse hair that, happily notwithstanding its inconvenient length, does not curl or kink. A dog of this breed is allowed a choice in colors. He may wear black with some white hairs interspersed, or he may indulge in fawn-color with black or dark-brown tips to the hairs, without really losing caste. Again, it will not be set down to his discredit if his coat is of light gray with black tips; and to blue he has an undoubted right. All of these colors are admissible, and which is the prettier and more desirable is a matter of individual taste.

Though the Skye is little and of peculiar shape, and though he is called a " toy," he is genuine dog all through. Full of life, a good watcher, intelligent, affectionate, peaceable in disposition, and not inclined to quarrel, and, above all, fond of children. To this list of attractions add that he is of strong constitution and fond of sport, that rats and other small destroyers of our peace incline to migrate when he sets up his kingdom, and that his coat is kept in order without much trouble, and all must agree that few can surpass him in desirability for the household.

No such sinecure is the care of the Yorkshire; and as to his qualifications for residence in a human family, opinions differ widely. For he is one of the dogs women are reproached with keeping who require more care than an average child. He must not only be washed and dressed and fed as carefully as a child, but in addition he must be thoroughly brushed and groomed, from the tips of his sharply trimmed ears to the end of his docked tail. He certainly, if any one of his race does, needs a special attendant, who can give an hour or two daily to keeping his coat in order, and as much more time to exercising him. One cannot help pitying the poor little fellow, for his coat must be the trial of his life, like long curls to the child who begins to be a " boy " before his mother is ready to give up her baby. He truly " must suffer to be beautiful." If his hair tangles, which it has a fatal tendency to do, he must submit to unlimited brushing; if he scratches himself—and what dog does not?—he is clad in mittens so that he cannot relieve his torture.

In color the typical Yorkshire should, first, have a muzzle of a deep shade of tan, without taint of gray or brown, and, secondly, a straight-haired coat of blue, also without adulteration. His legs should be tan, and his toenails black. His eyes must be dark and well set in his head; and beware lest he tips the scales at more than a dozen pounds. When the ordeal of his morning toilet is over, and the Yorkshire is well brushed and combed and put in order, he is eminently fitted to spend his day—or what is left of it—sleeping on a satin cushion in an upholstered dog-basket.

But the Yorkshire does not take the palm either for beauty or for care required to keep him in order. That belongs to the snowy bit of caninity named the Maltese. This creature is truly a martyr to beauty, a *"chien du luxe"* one writer calls him. His coat is very long and light, and silvery white in color. He can hardly move without tangling it, and a tangle

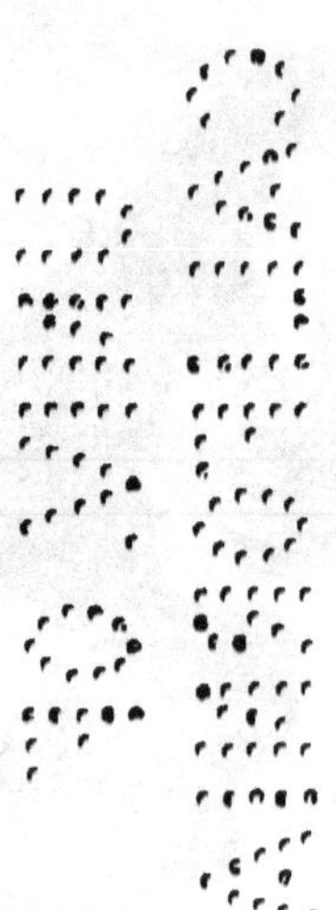

is a serious matter, requiring to be removed by drawing out one hair at a time. By no means dare one resort to so rude a process as brushing; indeed, so delicate is the texture that nothing more harsh than the softest baby's brush must ever be used on this dainty "creation" (to use the milliner's word that seems most appropriate to him). If he has the misfortune to get a spot on his precious coat, no vulgar washing must remove it; it must be cleaned as carefully as the most delicate fabric in madam's wardrobe. His regular bath is by no means a common washing; it is performed with a soft sponge, using a particular fluid made of fresh eggs and warm water, and administered with extraordinary care, to avoid tangles and colds, to which the pampered beauty is exceedingly liable.

The tail of the Maltese is beautiful as the caudal plume of the Persian cat, and is carried gracefully over the back, as the cat carries his. His weight should never be over six pounds. The whole animal looks more like a bit of bric-à-brac to adorn a drawing-room than like a dog. Yet the soul of the dog is there, intelligent and quick, affectionate and full of play, could he only be allowed to indulge in it. He is really as interesting as he is beautiful. The most scrupulous care must be exercised about his food. Little meat and no grease must go into his stomach. He cannot do without regular exercise, and—unfortunate creature!—he, too, must wear mittens. The Maltese is rarely seen in America, and can never be common anywhere.

The King Charles and the Blenheim spaniels are always beautiful and charming pets, whether they happen to be in fashion or not, and they have the advantage of not requiring such absolute and exclusive devotion that their mistress or their maid must sacrifice everything to their care. One may keep either of these dogs and still have leisure to read a little and entertain occasionally.

The King Charles should be a fine black with rich tan markings; the Blenheim white with markings of red. Both have round heads, snub-noses, and projecting foreheads; eyes large and dark and far apart; ears set far down and very long, with heavy fringe of hair. The hair of the body should be soft and wavy but not curly, and on the docked tail

very long and silky. The legs must be well
"feathered," the body short and thick, and
the dog should not weigh more than eight or
ten pounds.

More intelligent little fellows than these
two spaniels would be hard to find. They
delight in learning tricks and going of errands
about the house. They are devotedly attached
to their friends, and in every way desirable.
Furthermore, though they are not so fashionable as they have been sometimes in the past,
they are always winning, and they can never
be common.

The toy greyhound, however beautiful (and
he is like a fairy dog), is never, except in
very warm weather, a pleasant object to have
about, because he is always miserable and suffering with cold. He should wear a thick
blanket out-of-doors, and even then it is painful to see him shrink and shiver. His most
desirable color is clear fawn, of which there
are no fewer than four shades, golden, dove,
blue, and stone. Other colors are cream, red
or yellow, black, and mixed. In the fawn-
color should be no white markings of any description ; they detract greatly from his value,

and injure him for the " dog show," although they do not make him less dear to his mistress. This dog must hold his ears lying backward, and every pains must be taken with his diet in order to preserve his chief distinction —a slim figure. He is lively and interesting in the house, unusually affectionate and good-tempered, but not remarkably intelligent. He is also almost painfully timid, for which, by-the-way, he should never be punished, since it is a part of his nature over which he has no control. He is not very satisfactory as a pet, for he is always delicate in our climate, and needs particular care, such as bathing with a damp sponge only, followed by rubbing and careful wrapping up to prevent chill. He is himself so neat in the care of his coat that he does not need the rough scrubbing required by some of his fellows.

The newest thing in small house pets is the Japanese spaniel, or, as some call him, Japanese pug. So new is he, indeed, that he has not had time to become fashionable. He is graceful in form, with a snub-nose, large dark eyes, long hanging ears, and a tail curled up like a pug's. His coat is black and white in color, and soft as silk. He may be allowed to reach the weight of eight pounds, though if he can manage not to exceed three he is much more valuable. The aristocrat of the family — for there are degrees even in the "inner circle"—wears yellow instead of black to set off the white of his exquisite wavy coat. Both varieties are rare and costly even in Japan, and very difficult to procure. In the old days none but the highest nobles was allowed to possess one.

An interesting story was lately unearthed in Japan by the New York gentleman who has imported most of the race which have appeared in this country. According to the tradition, which is vouched for as true, so long ago as in the thirteenth century a Japanese nobleman took some of these dogs to England, and from them came the King Charles and Blenheim spaniels, which have held their own position to this day.

There are several of these dogs now living in New York, brought, it is said, from the Mikado's own kennels, one of whom does not weigh more than three pounds, is fifteen inches long, and worth fifteen hundred dollars.

This little Japanese is one of the most intelligent of his race, affectionate, and exceedingly sensitive. He is also very active, and altogether a most attractive pet — perhaps the "coming dog" about whom we have heard so much. He is dainty in taste, and delights to dine on tea-roses; but since at New York prices that would be rather extravagant, he will content himself with rice and chicken. He must have the softest of cushions, the most comfortable of quarters, and the best of care to flourish. Several of these dogs were on exhibition at the recent dog show.

What is called the toy black-and-tan is as nearly as possible a copy of his normal-sized relative, and, in fact, he is simply a dwarf, of course the smaller the better. One is said to have been raised that lived to be over two years of age, and measured but four and a quarter inches from tip of nose to tip of tail (the body being but two and a half inches), and three and a quarter from the ground to the tip of his ears. One can hardly conceive of a dog so minute. The round skull and bulging eyes of this unnatural little fellow seem, as one looks at him, to be pushed out of place by the crowding of the brain, and the effect is almost painful. Indeed, he rightly belongs to the "curiosities," and not in any way to the home dog of which these chapters treat.

XIX

THE HOME AND CARE OF THE DOG

ALMOST every individual has his own way of treating the pets of his household, from the thoughtless master who considers "anything good enough for a dog," to the traditional fine lady who provides her pet with an apartment of his own, containing every appliance for the toilet, and every article of adornment and luxury that can possibly be used about him, including a maid to attend to his needs. No one seems to think it involves a question of right and wrong, or that there is any moral responsibility attached to the keeping of pets; but I maintain that there is, and, further, that no one has a right to take into the household an animal who cannot speak for himself (at least so that the careless can understand) without giving thought and care to his comfort and health, and more to his happiness.

The middle course between the two extremes above cited is, as usual, the best. The dog as well as any other pet should be emphatically one of the family, and made as much at home, and as comfortable, according to his needs, as the master himself.

The first care should be to provide him with a regular sleeping-place, and a suitable bed and furnishings. The dog, as well as the man, enjoys the feeling of home given by a settled resting-place ; and no more than the man does he like sleeping "anywhere and anyhow," on the hard floor or the rough mat, as it happens, with no covering for cold nights. Pet dogs become accustomed to soft beds and their belongings, and learn to sleep quietly, and keep the covering over them. One whom I knew, when the cover slipped out of place in the night, used to go to the bed of his mistress, and waken her to have it replaced. One night when she was not well, and feared taking cold if she got up, she felt obliged to deny him, and he was so offended that he would have nothing to do with her for a day or two, refused food from her hand, and even took up his abode at a neighbor's house.

For a big dog, the home with its bed is

naturally in a kennel, shed, or some out-building. Wherever it is it should be dry, clean, and light, and protected from cold in winter. The floor should slope a little so that water will run off, and for the bed itself there should be a low bench or platform, on which is laid clean straw, fresh every few days, and covered by an old rug or bit of carpet, which is tacked down so that it will remain in position. The whole place should be kept clean and sweet by the use of whitewash or paint, and frequently washed out with a hose. The owner of a valuable dog will find his reward in the happiness no less than in the good health of his pet.

A dog of the medium size who sleeps in the house, as the cocker and other spaniels, as well as the black-and-tan, and his fellow-terriers, needs at least a corner of his own in a hall or empty room (never in a cellar), where his bed, a strip of carpet or something of the kind, shall be spread every night, and where, also, if he is troublesome by reason of wandering about the house, he may be chained up for the night.

The delicate dogs, the tender greyhounds

and the toys, need beds almost as soft and as well protected as our own, such as a half-covered dog basket, or a box of the right size with cushions and blankets. Letting a dog sleep in, or even on the bed with his master or his mistress is good for neither man nor beast, though it may be well to have him in the room, so that he can make it known if he needs attention in the night.

The question of the diet of a pet is, if one would keep him in perfect condition, as important as that of our own. At the same time, it is much more difficult to manage than our own, for it is almost impossible to harden the heart against the coaxings of a loving, winsome creature who is accustomed to share one's joys and sorrows ; and to yield and allow him to partake of the family food is certain, sooner or later, to ruin his health. With the big out-of-doors dogs it is easy to make rules and hold to them, but the pet who follows at one's heels, who understands the call to luncheon as well as any one, who sits up and "begs" so prettily, it requires a really Spartan firmness to resist, though it must be done or he will suffer.

The best plan for feeding is to make a law, and enforce it rigidly, that a dog shall never have a mouthful from the table. Let him have his regular eating time, and not immediately following the family meals, so that he will be hungry and expecting it when they eat. It is said that two meals a day are enough for a dog, and just before the family breakfast, and perhaps four or five o'clock in the afternoon, are convenient hours. Care should be taken that he does not eat so much as to grow fat, and that he has the proper kind and variety of food. It is a mistake to give table scraps alone, to stuff him with raw meat, or to starve him on bare bones. He should have a little cooked meat, not highly spiced, or bread soaked in gravy, some plain vegetables, and a mush of some cereal, all mixed together, and not so much of it that he can pick out the meat and leave the rest. A bone not so hard as to spoil the teeth is good to gnaw on occasionally.

The dishes from which a dog is fed should be as clean as one's own, and never of rusty tin or iron; earthen-ware is better; and what is left on them should be at once removed.

His drinking-water should be fresh, often replenished, and always where he can get it. The care required to insure all these things will be amply repaid by the health and spirits of the animal, and the mistress should at least oversee it herself, for the creature who cannot complain is apt to be imposed upon. The tiny pets require even more attention, and these it is never safe to leave to careless hands. Lean scraps from the table, with broken bread and potatoes or other vegetables, and a little gravy are admissible for them. The Yorkshire, and other long-haired dogs, must either be fed from the hand or have their locks tied back to prevent soiling. In no case should these dainty pets be allowed candy, sugar, cake, pastry, or other rich food. They like them, of course, so does a delicate child, but they are just as unsafe for the one as for the other.

Many mistaken notions prevail about the proper way to treat a dog. The world is growing in wisdom and humanity, and the old saying that "the more you beat them the better they be," is no longer believed to be true of the dog any more than it is of the woman who was included in the doggerel. The best authorities agree that a dog should never be whipped, or struck a blow more severe than a slap with the hand, and even that not over the ears, mouth, or abdomen, where a slight blow may do great damage. A dog is an intelligent being, and as sensitive to tones of voice, to reproof and praise, as a child. The voice alone is all that is needed to control him, and to bruise his body to reach his mind is as brutal and unnecessary with the one as it is now acknowledged by the wisest educators to be with the other. Moreover, it is very important that if a dog is to be punished in any way it should be immediately after the offence, so that he will perfectly understand what it is for. He is very quick to appreciate injustice, caprice, or cruelty, and he conducts himself accordingly. If he is properly punished for an understood fault he is penitent, and begs, in his way, to be forgiven; if too severely or without understanding, he resents it.

One who holds the lives of others in his hands must not forget that liberty is the breath of life to beast as well as to man, and every one, whether in city or country, should daily have as much of it as is consistent with the rights of others. To keep one of these restless fellow-creatures chained up day after day is terrible cruelty, and one cannot be surprised that the unfortunate captive grows cross and savage under the treatment. If he is a watch-dog only, and it is not safe to have him at liberty, it would be more humane to muzzle him, and let him have the run of the place, or a yard of good size.

To make an animal of the canine race agreeable as a house companion in the city necessitates bathing at least twice a month. Great care is required in the case of one of the smaller and more delicate sorts to avoid cold, such as wrapping at once in flannel, or rubbing and brushing till every hair is dry.

The training of a dog for the companionship of people is a subject worthy of a book. As a rule, the home pet gets very little training, and, like the child of a thoughtless mother, runs over everybody, and makes himself a nuisance to all persons except his doting mistress. It is so easy in the beginning to teach a dog to behave himself, and be a pleasure instead of a pest, that it is surprising how frequently this simple duty is neglected, and the pet allowed to rule the house, and make everybody in it uncomfortable.

Most of the illnesses of dogs may be averted by proper feeding, plenty of exercise, and frequent access to growing grass. When a valuable or cherished dog is really ill, the first thing to do is to secure the best medical advice possible — the family physician, if he is a man broad enough to be willing to prescribe for a dog; if he is not, the best really scientific veterinarian; though it is said that the dog's ailments are so much more like those of men than of horses that he may be doctored in the same way that a man is treated, and in ordinary cases home remedies may be administered. I can specially recommend the use of homœopathic remedies, as easily given, and working like a charm on all animals, from a canary-bird to a horse. If, however, others are preferred, it is well to remember that a big dog like a St. Bernard requires as much medicine as a human being, and a small dog much less.

One of the most common troubles to which

our four-footed friends are subjected is fleas, and though it may not be called a disease, it deserves treatment, both for his own sake and the sake of those among whom he lives. One way that is recommended by good authorities for the larger patient is to wash thoroughly with some good carbolic or dog soap, first making a thick lather all over him (being careful to avoid the eyes), then rinse off, or allow him to take a swim. Another way that is prescribed is to saturate a rag with kerosene, and rub it into his coat, then wash with soap and water. This, of course, must be done with great care, by daylight, and the oil thoroughly removed. A carbolic-soap bath is good also for eczema or mange. Worms and skin diseases beyond benefit by the above simple remedy should be treated by a physician or a veterinary; and if rabies is feared, the dog should be shut up where he cannot get at any one, and medical advice obtained. In most cases the trouble is due to causes which can be removed. All sick dogs should be kept quiet and not worried.

If any surgical operation has to be performed, even a simple one, like removing porcupine quills or sewing up a cut, it is no more than humane to save his suffering by putting him under the influence of chloroform.

XX

THE PERFECT PET, THE CAT

" Let Hercules himself do what he may,
    The cat will mew, and dog will have his day. "

THE use of the pet as an aid to health has not been considered as it deserves. No instinct is truer than that of the unmarried woman of lonely life to surround herself with pets. The companionship of cats and birds in solitary lives has unquestionably kept more people than we suspect out of the insane asylum ; and if friendless men took kindly to them, there would be fewer misers, drunkards, and criminals than there are now. It seems to be the divinely appointed mission of our furred and feathered friends, who never grow gloomy with care, never suffer from envy, ambition, or any of our soul-destroying vices, to make us forget our worries, to inspire us with hope, and hence with health. How can we despair so long as

> "Howe'er the world goes ill,
> The thrushes still sing in it"?

Give but a thought to the old-time "sickroom," silent, dark, overshadowed with gloom. Could we, if we tried, do more to induce depression, discouragement, and death? Happily we are learning that the mind has to do with the misdeeds of the body, and that there are no more valuable curative agents than cheerfulness, happiness, and hope.

But while we no longer shut out the blessed sunlight, the life-giving air, the genial friend, we have still neglected to bring into use all the helpers. What can better shake one out of his dismal depression than the antics of a monkey, at which one absolutely must laugh? What will so quickly dispel the "blue devils" as the chatter of a saucy parrot, or the pranks of a frisky squirrel? Keep the doctor and the drugs in the background (if you don't quite dare to discharge him), abolish sighs and long faces, bring in the pets, and make trial of the cheerful-thought cure.

A TABBY BABY

In this rôle the kitten is inimitable. Nothing can be so droll, and at the same time so graceful and altogether charming, as the frolics of two or three kittens.

"Poor pussy" we naturally call the cat. Do we know why? Is it not in instinctive recognition of the strange fact that this gentle beast is the most generally misunderstood creature in the world? His reserve, his self-reliance, his inextinguishable love of liberty, have earned for him a name totally unlike his real character.

And why, again, do we always give a cat the feminine pronoun? The Arabs have a tradition that when the first father and mother went out into the desert alone, Allah gave them two friends to defend and comfort them: for defence, the dog; for comfort, the cat. In the body of the dog he placed the soul of a brave man, in that of the cat the spirit of a gentle woman.

The old notion that puss is incapable of friendship and attachments would not be worth attention did we not see it repeated to this day, and insisted upon as a well-proven fact. The contrary is the truth. The cat is exceedingly fond of his friends, and generous in his conduct to other animals. He is, to be sure, not demonstrative, nor does he kiss the hand that beats him; and, as we go about in our blundering way, unless we are made uncomfortable by a show of affection, fairly forced upon us, as is done by the dog, we do not notice it, and conclude it does not exist. Puss does not express his emotions by barking, prancing about, and knocking one down; but his quiet rubbing against his friend, his gentle touch of the tongue, mean quite as much as the more noisy greeting.

The cat-mother's kindness to the young of other animals is notorious. She will adopt into her family and bring up with all the love and care she lavishes upon her own little ones, creatures so incongruous as chickens, ducks, foxes, squirrels, puppies, hedgehogs, and even rats. Moreover, she forms friendships of the warmest sort; not only with dogs and horses, but with turkeys and fowls, readily giving up her warm bed by the fire to share the cold quarters of her friend.

It has been commonly supposed that because a cat will not learn to do tricks like a dog he lacks intelligence ; whereas, the truth is, he is too knowing to be driven to learn. He is more like the apes, who—the Africans say—do not talk lest they be put to work. It is now known that if he chooses he can learn even more tricks than a dog, and go through them with greater precision, provided he is taught by kindness and coaxing. If struck he turns sulky; if frightened he will do nothing.

Nor do we appreciate the usefulness of the cat. In some parts of the world cats are trained to act as carriers, and then they bring a high price. In Spain they are made free of garrets, where most of the grain is stored. Every attic granary has its small door under the roof for their use ; the roofs of the city are given up to them for a promenade, and many of them never come to the ground in their lives. In storehouses where grain attracts mice, puss is monarch of all he surveys, treated with due honors, supplied with food and drink, and in every way made welcome. If the whole cat race should be annihilated, we in America would speedily be brought to appreciate the service we have despised.

The government of the United States maintains quite an army of cats, more than three hundred, it is said, for use in the Post-office Department. The duty of these public servants is to preserve postal matter and mailbags from rats and mice, which they do most effectually, because they are kept in good condition by proper feeding. Each postmaster in the larger cities is allowed a proper sum—in some cases as much as forty dollars a year—for "cat meat." Before cats were taken into service great loss was sustained from the teeth of the rodents, who thought nothing of boring through a pile of bags and letters in a single night.

XXI

CATS OF HIGH DEGREE

ACCORDING to the observations of a late traveller, the domestic cat is to be found in every country on the globe. In Oriental lands he is cherished, and in the West he is rapidly growing in popular favor, though he has always had warm friends, especially among brain-workers, to whom the noisy dog is a disturber. That the cat is certainly "looking up" is plainly indicated by the records of a recent cat show in London, where about one thousand (including kittens) were exhibited, and where as nice distinctions were made between varieties as are made in similar shows of dogs.

In the opinion of those who thoroughly know the cat, and appreciate his many valuable qualities, no pet is so charming, none so desirable in a quiet home. Graceful and beautiful to look upon, quiet and unobtrusive in manner, dainty in taste, he is as welcome in the study as in the drawing-room. No accident to the most delicate treasures of bric-à-brac marks his presence, no ear-splitting barks disturb the absorbed worker, no violent demonstrations put to flight the thoughts of the student. When a terrier captures a rat, it is with noise and bluster enough to rouse the whole household ; but who knows by any demonstration the moment that pussy pounces upon his prey? So long and so perfectly has the unappreciated creature performed his duty of guarding our property from rats and mice, that we can hardly imagine what would be our suffering without his services.

Most costly and most beautiful are the aristocrats of the tribe—the long-haired cats—of whom there are three distinct varieties, differing in form, color, and quality of coat, as well as in disposition and temper. They are the Angora, the Russian, and the Persian.

The first-named is brought from Angora, in western Asia, the region which also furnishes the remarkable goat of the same name. In its native land, as indeed everywhere, this beautiful beast is a cherished darling of fortune,

CATS OF HIGH DEGREE

beloved in the family circle, and held at an enormous value. This is particularly the case —indeed he is altogether beyond price—if he happens to be snowy white with blue eyes, and is blessed with perfect hearing, which, strange to say, a cat of the short-haired variety bearing this combination of coloring sometimes lacks.

The Angora cat, of whatever color, has a small, daintily shaped head, with a nose not too long, and eyes of a hue in harmony with his fur. His shapely ears are nearly buried in his thick fur, and end in a tassel at the tip, while his neck and head are almost as heavily maned as those of a lion. The fine long hair, which is the distinguishing feature of the species, is silky, with a slightly woolly quality, and every additional inch of length adds many dollars to his price. His tail is long and graceful, with hairs longest at the base, and gradually decreasing in length towards the tip, which curls a little upward. This cat is found in several colors. Next in value to the pure white is the solid black, with deep yellow eyes. Third in rating come the soft slate and blue shades, and a light fawn, also with yellow eyes. Other hues are red and gray, both light and dark, and a rich smoke-color.

The Angora cat of any variety is rare in this country, and correspondingly choice and costly. He is a personage of well-bred manners and quiet ways; his temper is good, and he is docile and affectionate. In a word, he exhibits the virtues and graces natural to the cat family, having never been soured by abuse or neglect, or made irritable by starvation. A cat whose value is set among the thousands is sufficiently precious to insure good treatment.

One unfortunate passion he has, which he delights to gratify, utterly oblivious of the price set upon him by his human protectors. It is a love of roaming, of solitary excursions, both in the country, where he explores the woods and fields and indulges his taste for hunting, and in the city, where it becomes necessary to watch him like a runaway child. So clever is the cat in accomplishing his ends, and so quick-witted to seize an opportunity, and so lithe and supple his body, that he will slip out beside a servant opening the door, or push a window a little farther open, and make his escape in silence and unobserved. Of course no fence will confine him an instant. With all his attractions, this famous Eastern beauty is not so intelligent and mentally alert as some of his short-haired brothers of the West, but the life of luxury to which he is destined demands not so much mental as physical gifts; in his case, certainly, "beauty is its own excuse for being."

The Russian cat, which is seldom seen in our country, is somewhat larger than the Angora, with a coat coarser and more woolly, and a tail neither so long nor so gracefully graduated in length of hairs. In color, this burly subject of the czar may be black, or a brown tabby; at least these are the two, and the only two, variations in which he has appeared at the West. Naturally but little is known of his character and disposition; but in the case of one who lived in England it is reported that he displayed some tastes more resembling the canine than the ordinary feline preferences. He insisted upon living with the dogs on the place, and accompanying them both in their exercise and their hunts, and he obeyed the orders and signals of the keepers exactly as well as the dogs.

The Persian cat is born to the happiest fate of any of his family, for, according to the tales of travellers, he is, in his native land, not only loved and cherished, not only well treated and admired, but thoroughly respected, and he has an acknowledged position and rights. In form the bewitching Persian does not greatly differ from the Angora, but the tail is much more effective, for the longest and the thickest-set hairs being at the tip, they form a magnificent plume, which the dignified owner carries proudly erect, waving in the air as he moves. In his splendid silky coat is not a trace of woolliness, and it clothes the graceful creature from the tips of his ears to the well " feathered " toes.

Unless some undreamed-of feline marvel shall yet be discovered, this animal must forever be regarded as the perfect flower of the domestic cat family. Not only does he easily surpass all his competitors in beauty and grace, but he possesses charms of disposition and manner and dignity of bearing; and while most affectionate and loving, is still self-respecting and independent.

The Persian may be seen in many colors.

Very beautiful is that shade technically called "blue," but perhaps more familiar to us as Maltese. A superb specimen of this color a few years ago lived royally in a house where I visited. She was named after a queen of old, and no royal personage ever bore herself more magnificently I am sure. One of very rich colors, also seen in New York, was a deep orange running to smoke-color. Nothing could be more exquisite to look at, though this mottled effect is not considered "the thing," and detracts greatly from the value of the wearer. The black Persian, with orange-colored eyes, is one of the rarest and most highly prized of the race, and the pure white is perhaps not second in estimation. There are also several varieties of tabbies, and in nearly every one the deep yellow eye is the most desired. The eyes should be large and full; the hair should line the ears and fringe the legs, and even the toes, of this beautiful beast.

The love of liberty is the ruling passion of the Persian, as it is of the Angora. Every one of the long-haired, indeed, delights in long, solitary tramps. It seems impossible to cure

them of the desire; and what a cat really desires he generally succeeds in getting, sooner
or later. To own one of these most attractive
and most costly pets in the city, where thieves
abound, is to live a life of constant anxiety
and watchfulness. Only those who have kept
guard over a sly and cunning human lunatic,
ever plotting to escape, can appreciate the
vigilance necessary for his safety. Yet, in
spite of this, so ornamental and so beautiful is
the gentle creature, that few who are able to
do so can deny themselves the pleasure of
owning one.

The curious Siamese cat, of which a few
specimens have been seen in the West, is
white and black or dun-color and black. The
favorite style of decoration is black muzzle,
ears, legs, and tail, with the remainder of the
body white or dun. It has eyes of blue or
rich amber-color, and is more singular than
beautiful. However, since it is said that the
only pure breed is kept in the palace of the
King of Siam, and it is difficult to get any to
import, it will no doubt be greatly desired,
and bring a high price. It is more delicate in
constitution than our own cats, affectionate

and timid, following its friends about as a dog
will do. The head of the Siamese cat should
be long from the ears to the eyes, and not too
broad, the forehead rather flat, and the eyes a
little oblique and surrounded by black. The
form should be delicate, graceful, and rather
long, and the tail short and thin. Some directions for the care of this foreigner are given
in Chapter XXIII.

14

XXII

THE COMMON PUSSY

THE beautiful and costly pets of the long-haired varieties are, in our country, beyond the reach of the majority of persons; but the common pussy, the friendly little creature, all mews and purrs and wriggles of affection, is accessible to every one, and should have an honored and protected place at every fireside. And this for several reasons. He is a pleasing object to look at, and we cannot have too much beauty about us; he is indispensable to protect us from rats and mice; and, more important than all, he is the most available subject on which to train children in humanity, justice, and unselfishness.

Moreover, Nature has not bestowed her choicest gifts upon the long-haired gentry of the feline race. For the less pretentious short-haired, she has reserved intellect, wisdom, and affection. The Angora and the Persian are beautiful, but in cleverness and keen observation they do not compare with their plainer contemporaries ; they are affectionate in a degree, but they are not capable of the depth of love that shines out of the eyes of a common pussy, whose confidence has been won by kindness and just treatment.

The history of the cat is strange and interesting. The human race itself has hardly passed through such vicissitudes, from worship and royal honors to the kicks and curses of the superstitious and ignorant. Having, however, passed from the heights to the depths, he is now coming to be more justly treated, neither as a deity nor as an outcast, but as a fellow-creature with rights like ourselves. In France the cat has not only a hospital, but a market. Even in New York some comfort awaits him, though the persecutions of the ignorant and the brutal put an end to an experiment that was intended to furnish the homeless with shelter and care. The kind hearts that originated the plan have found other ways to mitigate the hardships of cat life among careless, selfish, or cruel people. Kind, motherly women, it is said, sacrifice their own comfort, and go out at night, when alone the cat has some chance for peace and quietness, feed hundreds of the neglected and the abused, and help to a merciful death such as have suffered at the hands of men or dogs.

The short - haired, our common domestic cat, presents a bewildering variety of colors from which to choose the home pet. Most rare among them is said to be the male tortoise - shell, a variegation without mixture of white. To be perfect, this animal should be of a black-red and deep yellow in large, clear-cut patches, not in the least speckled or mixed up. His tail should be long and tapering, and his eyes yellow. This perfect type is seldom seen, and when found is of great value.

The tortoise-shell in combination with white is a beautiful creature, and exactly as valuable as the foregoing, except for rarity. The white should, like the colors, be distinctly defined, and confined to the breast, the under parts, the legs, and the nose. The eyes must be yellow.

The tabbies ! Who of us does not remember some dear pet or playmate of our childhood, whose stripes lent probability to the pretence that we delighted in—that he was a real tiger out of the jungle, such as we saw in pictures, yet who was just a plain gray tabby, the most common and the meekest of cats? Of this family there are several species.

The brown tabby has black stripes, with no white on the body. The eyes should be yellow, and the form slim and graceful, with round feet. This personage has the credit of being the most intelligent of his race, the most easily trained to tricks of all sorts—in a word, the regular "show" animal. He it is who appears in the troupes of "educated," or "performing," or "learned" cats. Notwithstanding his reputation as a public character, adulation has not spoiled him for domestic life. He is remarkable, even among his kind, for honesty and faithfulness; and his love of children, and endurance of their often troublesome attentions, cannot be surpassed. He is really the ideal family cat.

The red tabby gets his name from the color of his stripes, which are red upon a yellowish-brown ground. The word red, however, must be understood in the dealer's sense; it is the red of some dogs, not the red of a flower or a fruit. The character of the red tabby is good, and his intelligence fully up to the average of the short-haired.

The silver tabby is the beauty of his branch of the cat family, with black stripes on light blue or very pale Maltese color. Sometimes the stripes are dark gray on a shining silvery-gray ground, and a cat thus colored is very beautiful. He is rather small of his kind, but is very alert and intelligent.

Another variety of this group is called the leopard tabby, being spotted instead of striped, and rejoicing in topaz eyes. One of the most attractive cats, seen now and then, seems to be a mixture of the striped and the spotted, and for this reason, I suppose, he has no name, and no regular place in the list. But for the home, and as an ornament, he is far ahead of all others except the silver tabby. He is very dark gray and pure black in large spots, surrounded by broken stripes in a way that can hardly be described, but is exceedingly rich and beautiful.

In all the tabby family, white or any mixture, as of the spots and the stripes just mentioned, is considered undesirable, from a cat-

TABBY KITTENS

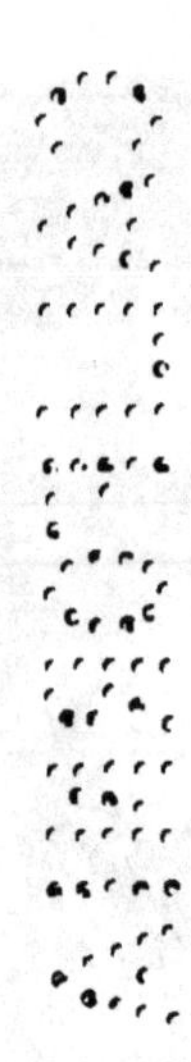

show judge's point of view, of course. In a houschold pet, destined exclusively for the family circle, these variations do not detract from the value.

The white cat, when perfect, is perhaps the greatest beauty of the short‑haired, but he must be absolutely perfect; for a draggled, thin, unkempt white cat is one of the most unattractive of the race. In the best condition he is elegant and graceful in shape, of a clear creamy white, with large blue eyes. Topaz eyes are next to the blue in beauty, while green are a decided blemish. It is a very common belief that blue-eyed white cats are always deaf. They are so sometimes, but by no means invariably, or even frequently. When well cared for, with fur immaculate, and body sufficiently plump, especially if he is adorned with a delicate tuft of silky hairs on the tip of a dainty ear, the white cat is a beautiful animal. It must be remembered, however, that a coat of that color is very hard to keep in perfect order, and washing and brushing are necessary to perfection. Even with this additional care the cat is not nearly so much trouble as a dog.

The black cat suffers from lingering superstition in the human mind, and great injustice has been done him on this account. I believe that Poe's horrible story in which he figures has also implanted in many people a feeling of repulsion they would hardly like to call superstition, yet which cannot be anything else. All this is exceedingly unjust to an innocent fellow-creature, who can no more help his color than we can ours. He is said to possess qualities finer than those of his fellows, being keener of hearing, greater in courage and spirit, and surpassing all others as a mouser. He is also more electrical than his congeners. To be perfect he must have yellow eyes, and fine silky fur without a white hair. One young lady of my acquaintance has had for a great many years a large family of black cats, keeping them pure by at once banishing any one showing a white hair. She declares them to be the most knowing and delightful of the race.

The Maltese, of many shades, from dark slate-color to an almost silvery hue, is always beautiful, intelligent, and good-tempered. To be perfect of his kind he should be a solid

color, without black or white, or any suspicion of stripes, and have a dark nose and yellow eyes. Any colored ribbon will "become his complexion," and he never ceases to please the eye.

It may be thought that any cat dressed in black and white will come under one of the technical titles black-and-white or white-and-black. But that is a mistake, for the perfect cat of either name is restricted to very limited and well-defined markings. The black-and-white is a black cat with white markings. The whole body clear black, with a white patch beginning between the eyes in a point, spreading to include the whole nose, descending upon the breast, and ending in a graceful curve at the bottom, the whole resembling the shape of a pear. The feet and pads may be white; the eyes must be deep yellow. His perfection is often marred by black nose and lips or black whiskers, either of which is a blemish.

The white-and-black is the reverse of the last named, in that it is white decorated with black, but it is less regular in markings. Sometimes the black appears in the ears;

again, the tail will be of that hue; this one
will show a black blaze on the face, and that
one will walk on black feet. He is, in fact, a
being of eccentricities. A very peculiar specimen was shown in a cat show, who had on the
back a perfect Maltese cross. Whatever form
the markings may take, they must be clear-
cut and even, that is, alike on both sides.

It is interesting to know that the charms of
the cat, and, above all, the irresistible fasci-
nations of the kitten, have been appreciated
·by some artists; but so great is the difficulty
of fixing in clay or upon canvas the infinitely
changing attitudes and expressions of the most
capricious and volatile of young beasts that
few have ever reached success. The greatest
of all painters of cats and kittens is a contem-
porary, and a woman, Madame Henrietta Ronner, of Brussels, and her pictures are marvellous reproductions of cat life. If we may
believe Ruskin, that to paint this beast it is
necessary to " know kitten nature down to the
most appalling depths thereof," then we may
safely assume that Madame Ronner is a cat-
lover, for no one really knows a cat who does
not love him.

XXIII

THE CARE OF THE CAT

THERE are among civilized people two strange but almost universally prevalent errors about the cat: first, that if he is fed he will not catch mice, and second, that he attaches himself to places and not to people.

In consequence of the first notion thousands of the unfortunate creatures are kept almost at the point of starvation, and as a natural result are too spiritless and miserable to be good mousers. This mistake, for it surely is one, should be combated on every occasion by the cat-lover, who must never tire of repeating that a half-starved cat is not a successful hunter, while to a well-fed beast the pursuit of his legitimate prey is "sport" for which he is always ready.

Whoever wishes to have the family cat in good condition, to keep the house clear of mice, to play with the children, to be a credit

to his owner, must see that he has good food
and care, and that he is made contented and
happy. He can exist without these conditions, but he will be a different beast. An
eminent naturalist, and a lover of the cat, says
that "one who owns a cat should treat it as if
it were his child, be thoughtful of its wants,
encourage its affections, be kind but firm in
his prohibitions, and watchful for its peculiar
traits of character."

In regard to diet. A cat should have sweet
milk to drink, and water, always fresh and
clean, where he can get it if he desires. He
needs meat once a day, and it should be
mixed with some vegetable, such as asparagus,
of which he is very fond, cabbage, or some
other that he likes. Fish is not indispensable
in pussy's menu. He likes it, to be sure, but
not so much more than meat as he is popularly
supposed to do. Raw meat is good for him,
but it must always be accompanied by vegetables. One meal a day is said to be enough
where there is a chance for successful mous-
ing, but a family pet who sees his human
friends eating three times, is apt to consider
himself entitled to the same number of meals.

Kittens need food three times a day. They should have meat cut very small, and bones to gnaw, and their milk should be warmed by adding a little hot water. Their principal food should be boiled rice, brown bread or oatmeal with milk, and boiled vegetables, alternated from day to day, for animals like variety as well as men. Both the cat and the cat's baby are fond of catnip.

The food of the Siamese cat is, in his native land, fish and rice boiled together, but he has been kept in England without fish. The kittens are hard to raise, and all through life this species requires peculiar care.

It seems hardly necessary to say that the home pet should have plenty of fresh air, and all the sunshine he can get, but it is imperative that something should be said about the sleeping-quarters. It is a surprising fact that many persons deliberately and regularly turn the family cat out of doors for the night. The poor beast is thus forced to become a vagabond, to make night hideous with his yowls; to sleep where he finds shelter, and to keep himself from freezing the best way he can. Certainly there are many kind-hearted people who have never reflected upon the straits they thus force upon a beast they may even be fond of. But whether fond or not, there is a moral obligation on the part of one who takes a help- less animal into the family to see that it is comfortable, and also that it is not an annoy- ance to the neighbors.

The cat should always have a bed, warm in winter and cool in summer. If he is allowed to enjoy his back-fence promenade during the evening, any well-treated cat will be glad to come home at bedtime, unless he has been made a confirmed vagabond by former neg- lect. In that case he can soon be cured by forming the habit of giving him some dainty just at bedtime. A round basket, with clean straw or a bit of carpet, makes a good bed. A warm cellar is a comfortable place, and a bar- rel, prepared like the basket, is a convenient bed. If he sleeps in the kitchen or sitting- room, it is well to have a box of dry earth be- side his quarters. No living creature should be shut into a closet or cupboard for a night; fresh air is the life of beast as well as man.

A well-kept cat is the pink of neatness, for- ever washing and brushing his fur. The short-haired almost invariably keep themselves in perfect order, but to the long-haired this is a herculean task. They require washing and brushing.

To bathe a cat is a delicate operation, and requires tact. He is exceedingly nervous and sensitive, and he shrinks from water. He must be handled like a delicate child, with slow and gentle movements, and the constant encouragement of a voice he knows and trusts. It is best to have a helper in the work, one to talk to and pet the frightened creature, while the other puts him slowly and carefully into blood-warm suds, pressing but not rubbing the long hairs, and rinsing in the same gentle way in another tub. He must then be wrapped in a blanket, and dried before a fire with warm towels, and not be allowed on the floor until thoroughly dry and glowing.

If the long hair of one of these beauties gets tangled or matted together, it should first be moistened with oil, or soft-soap and a little water, and then separated with the fingers, pulling the hairs out of the tangle one by one, after which must follow the washing. The peculiar wavy beauty of the hair and its natural way of lying will not endure the roughness of a comb, or even a brush, except a soft one.

More than any other beast the cat needs gentle treatment. Ages of persecution have made him suspicious, and it will require ages of kindness to eradicate that trait from his character. He is, therefore, on the lookout for injustice and cruelty; a rough word makes him shrink as from a blow; harsh reproof strikes upon his sensitive nerves with terrible effect. He must be won by gentleness and loving care before he will be convinced of the friendship of a human being and be his natural self; and he must not be blamed for it either; it is the fault of the race which has so long ill-treated him. He cannot, like the dog, take good-will for granted, because the whole experience of his life teaches him otherwise.

His confidence won, however, no pet is so delightful in a quiet-loving home as the cat, and the difference between one thus treated and the ordinary beast is marvellous. "His gestures and actions," says Rev. J. G. Wood, describing his own pet cat, "are full of that spirited yet easy grace which can never be at-tained by any creature, be it man, beast, or bird, who has once learned to crouch in terror, and to fear a harsh tone or an uplifted hand." And, further, "the fearless, confiding movements, the clear, open glance, and intelligent expression of a well-treated cat are so different from the furtive, scared look of a poor animal that is hunted about and kicked out of the way, that the two seem hardly to belong to the same species. The wild savage, whose education is a perpetual distrust of everybody and everything, is not more unlike the high-born and accomplished European gentleman than an ill-used cat unlike one treated kindly."

Their confidence won, the individuality of cats is marked; they differ as greatly as children, and should be treated accordingly. I had in my home at one time two cats so nearly alike that without seeing the face and its expression they could not be told apart. They were Maltese, with silvery tips to their exquisite fur. One was emphatically an aristocrat, who lived in the parlor, slept by preference on a satin-covered mantel, and was most dainty in her tastes and manners; the other, equally well treated, took naturally to the kitchen, and was happiest there.

The above-quoted good friend of the feline race, who has often used his pen in their service, advises that if a cat needs correction it should be given in such a way that it will appear to be the natural result of his deed, and not a punishment at the hands of man. For example, a cat was cured of killing chickens by having one he had killed securely bound into his open mouth, and kept there for some time.

It is a bad plan to let a cat go out with a collar or a ribbon on. It is apt to catch in something and choke the wearer. I have known of one or two deaths by hanging from this cause. In the case of the long-haired, too, it wears and breaks the beautiful frill around the neck.

To keep this charming pet in health it is well, in addition to proper food and air and a comfortable bed, to have a pot of growing grass where it is always accessible, at least in city homes, where the natural article is not always to be found.

If a cat is really ill, he should be treated as a human patient is treated, kept quiet and warm, and have medicine suited to his disorder. The most convenient and easily administered, as I mentioned in the case of the dog, is the homœopathic. To insure the swallowing of doses having an unfamiliar or unpleasant taste requires tact and some labor. The animal must be wrapped up closely, so that he cannot use his claws to protect himself from what he considers an outrage, his mouth opened, the medicine poured down, and his head held up till the dose is swallowed, and the excitement of all this is apt to aggravate his illness.

An English lady who is learned in cat-lore, and has written a book upon the subject, recommends for delirium and fits a gentle aperient, and I will add that one can be brought out of a fit with ether or chloroform.

For distemper, which begins with vomiting of bright yellow frothy liquid, give at once an emetic, such as salt and water (or the homœopathic equivalent). After the salt and water has served its purpose, a soothing dose is advised of half a teaspoonful of melted beef marrow, free from skin, and not too hot. It may be necessary to repeat this treatment.

In "cat-pox," in which the hair falls off, should be administered a cooling diet and plenty of grass, while the spots are rubbed with flour of brimstone mixed with lard which has no salt. This will cure eruptions, and as the patient licks it he will swallow some, which is also good. I think it is the Irish who give medicine to a cat by daubing it on his coat where he can lick it off.

If a cat is hopelessly ill or injured, or if for any reason it is desired to be rid of him, the only humane thing to do is to take his life, provided that it is done in a painless way. A few cents' worth of chloroform, with which a sponge or cloth is saturated and held close to his nose, will very soon put the unfortunate into his last sleep. If one demurs at performing this last kindness to poor pussy, the same sponge placed with the animal in any tight vessel, like a common wash-boiler or covered tub, and closely shut up, will have the same effect in a little longer time.

It is a cruel thing to take a whole litter of kittens away from the mother at once. It should be done gradually, or else one left for her to bring up. Putting the cat's feelings out of the question, her physical system suffers.

I cannot close the subject of our treatment of the cat without a protest against an unkindness, to say the least of it, which we see perpetrated every summer. How many families do we see in the city who pack up their belongings and depart, bag and baggage, children, servants, and even dogs, and turn the key upon the family cat, who has just as strong a claim on them as the dog, just as much right to be provided for as he. Do they ever give a thought to the abandoned wretch, forced to spend his days on back fences, his nights where he can; to have no shade from the heat, no refuge from street boys, no water to drink, and to steal or starve through the long summer months, while the family are enjoying themselves in the country? Let nobody say the cat would not go. If well treated, and therefore fond of the family, he would be glad to go, and it would be far kinder to put the beast forever to sleep with chloroform than to abandon him to the life of a vagabond.

Moreover, besides the Society for the Prevention of Cruelty to Animals, which in our larger cities will mercifully dispose of inconvenient pets, there is now, at least in New York, a summer boarding-house for cats, and almost every family knows some person who would gladly care for the animal through the summer for so small a sum as twenty - five cents per week. It fairly rends the heart of a friend of the gentle beast to see the homeless, suffering, starved specimens of cathood that haunt the area doors and the back yards, half dead and wholly wretched, through the summer months of rest and travel.

XXIV

THE MONKEY TRIBE

THE most desired and the most dreaded of pets belongs to the race nearest the human in many ways, our next of kin—the four-handed. Monkeys of all sorts, from the tiny specimen who can hide between one's two hands up to the savage gorilla himself, have been eagerly sought as pets since the beginning of time, or at least as far back as we can find out how people lived.

While our four-handed relatives are the most amusing, they are, also, unfortunately, the most troublesome of pets. The addition of one of them to a family circle is almost invariably the cause of dissension. He is the pet lover's delight, but just as certainly the house-keeper's despair. The one feels that it is cruel to confine to a cage a creature so active and restless, while the other bemoans the furniture injured, the bric-à-brac destroyed—

in fact, the insecurity of any object under the roof with that mischief-working creature. The one and the only way, therefore, to satisfy both factions in the household, is to place the cunning culprit in a room by himself, in which is nothing he can injure, and let him visit the other parts of the house only under the guardianship of some one who can give undivided attention to him, and who shall be made responsible for any pranks in which he may indulge.

Monkeys are in several respects delightful pets. They are so intelligent that a study of their ways is of great interest; they are always original, even in their naughtiness, and so comical in their doings that they furnish a never-failing source of entertainment to the grown-up part of the family, while to the children they are the most charming of playmates. A chimpanzee who played with children would imitate everything they did in their games, and when they resorted to "making faces" to amuse themselves, they found that he could beat them at that. He understood that it was in play, and seemed to take as much pleasure in it as they did. No house can

IN MISCHIEF

be very dull that enjoys the presence of a monkey.

Besides this, they are affectionate little creatures; they form the warmest friendships with people, sometimes even becoming almost painfully attached to a friend. They are sensitive, too; they respond readily to kindness; they grieve over our neglect, and resent being ridiculed or laughed at. One monkey felt so insulted by a gentleman going about on all-fours, which he evidently considered as intended to mock him, that he went into a fury of rage, and never forgave the joker, with whom he had previously been on the most friendly terms.

That all of the four-handed are mischievous, Dr. Oswald (who has given much study to them) says is a mistake. The most fertile in troublesome pranks belong to the African branch of the family, though it must be admitted that our own monkeys are not above reproach in that regard; they will all, as our grandmothers used to say, "bear watching."

The first and the most imperative duty of a keeper of one of these lively pets is to furnish plenty of entertainment for him—objects that he may hammer and bang, and toys that he may destroy; for what is called mischief is simply his irrepressible activity. He must be doing something; he has no genius for repose. Hence it is cruel to keep a monkey in a cage, not only because he is a pitiable sight to every one who loves his own freedom, but because he will pine and die for want of something to interest him. A monkey made happy, kept comfortably warm, and properly fed so as to be in health, is a perennial source of interest and amusement in a household. There is no end to the stories of these comical fellow-creatures, with their drolleries and almost human ways, from Du Chaillu's quaint baby *Nshiego Mbouva* down to the pathetic little fellow on the hand-organ whose heart Mr. Garner won by addressing him in his own language.

Perhaps the most civilizable monkey that we can get at is the spider monkey, from Central America. This fellow takes kindly to our ways of living, is neat and nice in person, exceedingly affectionate, and often most gentle in disposition; though animals differ in characteristics exactly as people do. In buying a pet, therefore, it is important to select one

that is naturally amiable, whose temper has not
been soured by ill-treatment. When washed
and brushed every day, the spider monkey becomes really beautiful, and his golden-brown
coat silky to the touch. He readily learns to
walk on two feet, or hands, which makes him
about two feet tall, and he has so many ways
of expressing his mind that he may be almost
said to talk.

The only objection to the spider monkey is
his size. He is rather large for a home pet;
but hundreds of smaller ones are brought to
our seaport cities every year, and may at any
time be bought of the dealers in beasts and
birds. There is not one of them, I believe,
unless his temper has been sorely tried by
abuse, who will not be easily tamed by kindness and care, and become a source of great
pleasure to his keeper.

As I said, this restless creature should never
be caged; but it is necessary to have some
way of limiting his range, and perhaps the
least irksome is by a light chain, not heavy
enough to be a burden, and long enough to
give him some liberty. Changing his place
from time to time, now attaching his chain to

the kitchen-table leg, now to a clothes-post in the yard; for an hour chaining him where he can look into the street, and for another where family affairs may interest him, will give him the variety he craves, and keep him interested and amused.

This shivering exile from the tropics should always have a warm and comfortable bed, with plenty of blankets or other coverings. A dry and airy furnace-room is a good place for him to pass his nights; but it must be dry, for he is exceedingly susceptible to cold and dampness. A small hammock, or a swing of proper size, will furnish him amusement for hours every day.

As to diet, the monkey needs very little or no animal food, but plenty of grain products and fruit. He is particularly fond of eating what his human friends eat, and he develops a discriminating taste very quickly. Nothing delights him more than to take his meals at the family table, where he will go through the bill of fare, from soup to coffee, with the greatest relish.

The smaller members of the four-handed tribe, the marmosets, are much more easily kept in the city, and if one is careful to secure a pet of a gentle disposition, he will be found as harmless in the house as a domestic pussy. He is neither so restless nor so mischievous as his bigger brethren; nor, it must be added, is he so intelligent and interesting to study. A marmoset who is well cared for, washed and brushed, and properly fed, is a delicate and dainty pet that no lady need hesitate to have about her person; and to be close to a human being, cuddled into the neck above one's collar, or snuggled down in a warm hand, is the dearest delight of the shivering little creature, who suffers much in our climate.

I said the little beast was as harmless as pussy. I should qualify that statement by making one exception. The marmoset is apt to be unfriendly to a bird. He seems to regard a canary as his legitimate prey, and the more spirited of the family will attack any caged bird.

In buying one of these little fellows out of a store or from a sailor, the first thing to be looked after is a tight band, which it is customary to tie around the body to attach a cord or chain to. Very often this band is uncomfortably tight, perhaps because the animal has grown, and his fur is apt entirely to conceal it. I have known more than one made very cross and nearly killed by this band, who on being relieved of it changed greatly for the better both in health and temper.

Marmosets living under conditions so unnatural are extremely delicate, and need thoughtful care, first as to food, which should be mostly fruit, with bread and oatmeal or other grain if they like it; and secondly, though perhaps even more important, as to warmth. A marmoset prefers to be about the person of his keeper. I knew one that was perfectly happy in a round knitting-ball basket hung from his mistress's belt, and another who spent nearly all his time in the breast-pocket of his master's coat. A completely equipped doll's cradle furnished one pet with a comfortable nest by day and bed by night, and he would slip under the covers as deftly as anybody.

A marmoset that I kept myself lived comfortably all winter on a mantel against a chimney which a furnace fire kept always warm, in a room that was never cold. The mantel was covered with a board wrapped in flannel, and

he was fastened by a light cord to an iron
weight, the cord having a swivel so that it
would not kink. The cord was long enough
to give him the freedom of the mantel, a tall-
backed chair at one end, and a bookcase at the
other.

The bed of my pet was a wooden box lined
with blanket, with a piece of the same spread
over the top for cover; and the care with
which he lifted the blanket, curled his tail up
like a watch-spring, and slipped in so as not
to disarrange the covering was very droll to
see. In spite of all this warmth, if I heated a
flat stone and put it on the mantel, he would
discover it in a moment, take his seat on that
stone, and never leave it till all the warmth
had departed.

A pair of marmosets that lived in a house
in Brooklyn were kept in a large cage, perhaps two and a half by four feet, and four
feet high. The bed was in a small box fastened up under the roof, with a small round
hole for entrance. During the summer they
were kept on a back porch, and after getting accustomed to the surroundings they
were let out every day. At first they were

afraid to leave the porch, but they soon grew bolder, and made excursions all about the vicinity, using the cat's highway, the back fences. Dogs always barked at them, but from dogs they were safe; but I was not so sure about cats till I was amused to see that pussy plainly regarded the droll little beasts as uncanny, and gave them the right of way whenever they appeared.

About four o'clock every day the little wanderers returned to their cage and to their bed for the night. Excepting when their cage door blew shut, or somebody was too near it when their sleeping-time arrived, I believe they never failed to go home. Two years the little fellows furnished amusement and interest to the neighborhood by their pranks.

XXV

ODDITIES

THERE are some interesting pets to be found among what are called the half - monkeys— animals that are really four-handed, but differ in other respects from the Simian race. Many of these, and other strange little creatures, find their way to our ports as the pets of sailors, who are much given to buying all sorts of oddities in foreign lands.

Two of the four - handed, who were kept with comfort and safety in a parlor, were a kinkajou and a lemur. The first-named was from Central America, a pretty little fellow about the size of a cat, with golden-brown fur, a long prehensile tail, and large expressive eyes. He slept all day, and came out at dusk to eat and frolic during the evening, such being his habit in his native woods. His food was bananas, and his manners were gentle, though quaint and playful, and he was a most enticing pet.

The second of the parlor pets was a lemur —the black-handed lemur from Africa—and he was a born rogue, as full of pranks and drolleries as a monkey. He was also about the size of a cat, with dark-brown woolly fur and a long tail, by which he did not object to being carried. He, too, was half nocturnal, sleeping all day, and coming out at night for his exercise.

By some contrivance as to quarters, and about an hour's daily care, both of these little animals were kept safely and agreeably to the household. Though they were at liberty in a parlor from about four o'clock till ten every evening, they did no harm, because their keeper was always there. No monkey or other pet ever furnished more amusement to a family than they did. Neither of them cared to eat anything but banana, and that only in the evening.

Another interesting pet is the nasua, or coati, or nose-bear, from the tropical regions of our country. He is very comical in looks, as his name suggests, and is one of the most common pets in his native land. He is amusing and affectionate, readily adopts our bill of fare, and especially delights in eggs. He makes himself useful as a destroyer of rats and mice and cockroaches. This little creature is not nocturnal, and should not be kept in a cage, but have the run of the house. He is not mischievous.

Another South or Central American is the armadillo, the small variety called ball-armadillo. He is entertaining and droll, and if allowed the run of a yard in summer he will find his own food, as ants and small insects form his menu. In winter he must, of course, be fed.

Other foreigners whom we see occasionally in our Northern homes, and who are very common as pets in their native country, are ocelots and jaguars. Both are intelligent and winning. In fact, the young of any beast may be tamed and domesticated ; they may be taken very early and brought up on the bottle, which is the safest way with those mentioned, as well as with bears, wolves, lions, or tigers. They are very satisfactory while young and playful, but as it is not always safe to keep full-grown ocelots and panthers, it is cruel to accustom one to domestication, to being fed and cared for, and then to abandon him to his own resources. It is hardly less unkind to subject him to the discomforts of life in a menagerie, at least if he is large.

This consideration—the question of what to do with the pet grown up and not suitable for petting—makes it undesirable to take any of the larger animals from their natural surroundings. The young grizzly bear, for example, is a bonny little beast, gentle and affectionate, and full of funny antics; but a full-grown grizzly, though ever so amiable in disposition, is a terror to every one except his master, and, with the best intentions, his immense power makes him a dangerous neighbor.

We have, however, many little animals in our country pleasant for pets, and not too large to be kept when of full size and strength. I should hardly include in the list, however, one who is a great favorite and a very bewitching infant — the fox. He is nearly as funny as a monkey, but in spite of the best training his taste for poultry, and especially for wildness, is ineradicable; and the person who sets his heart on a tame fox is sure to come to grief some day by finding his pet become a savage hunter of chickens and turkeys.

More amenable to civilization are the raccoon—or coon, as popularly called—the opossum, the prairie-dog, and others, besides the most common of pets, the rabbit and the guinea-pig. The raccoon has long been a favorite pet. He is intelligent, fond of fun, and loves to frolic with children, whom he never harms. He is personally neat, and readily becomes so thoroughly domesticated that he loses all desire for freedom. This, of course, when he is well fed and cared for, and not caged. He will eat anything from the table, and is often fond of coffee to drink. He is somewhat inquisitive, it must be confessed, and will now and then treat himself to something out of the pantry, pulling out a cork and uncovering a jar as handily as if he had done it all his life. Therefore, a pet coon must be locked out of the provision-rooms.

The opossum is another pleasing little fellow, who, being sharp-witted and knowing, will look out for his own comfort. When young he is, like all animals, fond of play, but he does not usually become so much attached to people as do some other of our little friends. Moreover, he has the bad habit of using his teeth too freely, chewing up slippers and handkerchiefs and anything else he can get hold of.

Taken young, the prairie-dog is a most fascinating pet, lively and droll, as tame as a cat, and fond of being petted. He will eat almost any vegetable food, and the only trouble to be feared is his fondness for gnawing and burrowing. He is neat and nice to have about the house, but he is happier to have the run of a yard, and dig out a home for himself under the sod.

An unusual pet, but, according to Dr. Hart Merriam, one of the most agreeable, is the common skunk. He is, to begin with, a beauty, being black and white, with long glossy fur, and a beautiful bushy tail tipped with white. He is lively and amusing, neat in habit, and most amiable. In regard to his too-well-known odor, Dr. Merriam, who has kept several of them, and knows them under all circumstances, says that when one is well

treated and made a pet of he never dreams of
exhibiting his peculiar accomplishment of per-
fuming a house. It is his means of defence,
and is used solely for that purpose. Boys
who wish to keep this pet must take notice
that worrying and teasing will probably be
promptly resented in a way they will not enjoy. Dr. Merriam's particular pet rode about
the country in his pocket, accompanied him
on foot when he walked, and delighted very
specially in hunting grasshoppers. Another
that I have heard of was kept in a family for
two years, and was not only a lively playmate
for the children, but an excellent mouser.
Now here is a pet that any country boy can
capture, and he will be rare as well as pleasing.

There are several other little animals native
to our country that have been kept as pets.
One such is the badger. Though not very
beautiful, with his long body and short bandy-
legs, he is good-tempered and lively, acting
much like a young puppy, especially in his
fondness for chewing and tearing things to
pieces. He is playful with children, and he
likes to go into the fields with his master,

where he regales himself on beetles and worms.

The young deer or fawn is a most winning pet, though he is exceedingly timid, and must be very gently treated. The disadvantage of this, as of other agreeable young animals, is that petting is inconvenient when they are grown.

The same objection exists to petting kids and lambs, both of whom are attractive, especially the kid, who is one of the most amusing and droll creatures in the world. A grown sheep or goat would be a somewhat inconvenient follower, and it is wiser not to cultivate their too intimate friendship.

Several foreign animals that we sometimes find in our stores are desirable pets. From Europe we get the hedgehog, a most comical little fellow, who rolls himself into a ball of prickles when he is offended or frightened.

From Australia come two delectable little beasts, the Australian opossum, who differs materially from ours, and the wombat, a funny little fellow, something like a baby bear.

The most absurd animal to pet, yet one

whom its friends declare to be most amusing
and most loving, is a pig. Of course, it is a
young one; but as it is a pity to have to give
up one's pet to live in a pigsty, this surely
cannot be a particularly desirable inmate of
our homes.

XXVI

SOME PECULIAR PETS

SOME of the most pleasing pets are found among the rodents, the little fellows whose teeth are so troublesome and require so much looking after.   There are the squirrels, to begin with.   Every one is frolicsome, neat, easy to take care of, and altogether bewitching. A squirrel of any sort likes a warm bed, out of the reach of meddlesome children, plenty of nuts to eat, and liberty—for, like everybody else, he hates a cage.   The gray squirrel is the most elegant of the tribe (unless we except the black, who is not so often seen), and he is intelligent and affectionate.   The red squirrel is one of the most lively of a wonderfully active family. and is exceedingly inventive in pranks. The chipmonk, though frisky enough, is said to be the least interesting of his race, and the flying-squirrel is rather quiet for one of his kind, and entertaining only at night.

As hinted above, all rodents require close watching, for their teeth grow rapidly, and something to gnaw is a necessity of their existence. This, indeed, is one reason why captivity in a cage is so distasteful to them—it is impossible to secure sufficient exercise for their teeth. The whole family is said to be unusually fond of music; some of them become so absorbed in listening to the notes of an instrument, or even to whistling, that they lose consciousness of danger, and may be caught without trouble. I would not advise, however, that one's hand be employed to seize a squirrel, for he might come to his senses and use his teeth.

Another rodent, the rat, is not popular with pet lovers in general; but persons who have overcome the repugnance which our race feels for his—Frank Buckland, of England, for instance—insist that he is, above all other little animals, amusing and entertaining. He is full of gambols as a kitten, and scrupulously neat in the care of his person, washing and brushing his fur as carefully as a cat. Though not over-dainty in feeding when he is wild and has to live by his wits, he is particular and notional to the last degree when he is cared for and able to choose his food. The rat is peculiarly amenable to instruction, readily learns to perform tricks of all sorts, and, what may seem most singular in one against whom every man's hand is raised, he becomes warmly attached to the friend who cares for him.

The white rat is often kept by boys, more, however, as a curiosity than as a pet, and always under protest from their mothers. But boys lose interest in it, and do not like care, so the poor creature is apt to be neglected and become an offence in the household. This need never occur with any rat that is cared for, especially if he is not confined to a close cage. The white rat is neither so intelligent nor, in my opinion, so pretty as his brown relative. The black-and-white rat of Japan is sometimes seen in our country, and he is said to resemble our own rats in his characteristics.

A winsome pet is the common brown mouse; and now I fancy I hear the most vigorous protests from my readers, who, though they do not shriek and take refuge on chairs and tables like Howells's feminine characters, still have a strong feeling of distaste to him. Nothing can be imagined more dainty, graceful, and altogether captivating than the tricks and manners of this humble resident within our walls. Once allay the poor little creature's fears of his big, clumsy, human proprietors, and his delightsome qualities are apparent. Frisky in movement, droll in conceits, and eccentric of action, he is a never-ending source of entertainment. Moreover, he is as teachable as the rat, absolutely neat in his ways, and most loving to his friends.

A singing mouse—which is not so great a rarity as one would suppose from the newspaper fuss that is sometimes made over one—has an added attraction as a pet. The singing is no doubt similar to that of the marmoset, and resembles the canary song a good deal smothered.

All these little creatures should be tamed, and attached to people by their affections, and not kept as prisoners in a cage. In the former case they display their peculiar characteristics, and take perfect care of their coats, while in the latter they require constant watching and attention, and show no individuality whatever.

It is not a pet that is kept in a cage, it is a prisoner, and a prisoner in his unnatural and unhappy life can never afford much pleasure.

Whatever beast is kept, it should have its own quarters, in which it is at home and free from intrusion, and to which it can retire when it chooses. This home should be kept clean and sweet by frequent changes of bedding and the use of soap and water. No one has a right to keep an animal in confinement who finds it too much trouble to attend to its health and comfort. It should be regularly fed on food that is most healthful for it, and, what is quite as essential to its happiness, and consequently to its health, it should be talked to and noticed as much as anybody. I am certain many animals and birds suffer and die in our homes from pure loneliness, and from being regarded by their human neighbors as creatures of an altogether different nature. Whereas the truth is, if one will but cultivate their acquaintance, he will be astonished to see how the dullest and most stupid will wake out of its apparent torpor, and show understanding and character. I know a family very fond of pets, in which the creatures show most extraordinary individuality. Their cats do things no cat was ever before known to do; their parrots and other birds show what we call human nature in a wonderful degree, and their dogs almost talk. The reason is plain: the animal or bird is made one of the family; it is talked to and petted as well as cared for; its intelligence develops, and the beast becomes very like the human being. Watched with loving eyes, the actions of the pet are understood and responded to, and one is surprised to see almost a common language established between the two races. It is a wonderful and beautiful study, and that family has more pleasure and real companionship with its pets than any other I know.

The least attractive of the animal world for pets are the reptiles, yet boys especially appear to dote upon them; possibly they are the easiest to secure. Where is the boy who never kept a turtle?—very uncomfortably, too, as a rule. If these unresponsive, cold-blooded fellows must be kept, they should at least be made as comfortable as possible. To be strictly just, too, though reptiles are harder to understand than the races more near to us in their nature, they do show intelligence, and even affection.

The alligator, which accompanies home nearly every traveller to Florida, and often performs the journey by himself in a box by mail, should have both water and dry land, so that he can choose for himself where he will abide. I have seen one kept in a tub of water unchanged till it was offensive, and another who had absolutely no access to water at all. Both these treatments were improper and cruel. A good way to make an alligator comfortable—which we are bound to do if we snatch him from his home and deprive him of liberty—is to prepare a large box that will hold water, with a board running up out of the water that he can occupy if he desires. A little pile of rocks, behind or within which he can hide, will be a welcome addition to his quarters. For food, place oysters or cut raw beef where he can get it. He usually prefers to eat in solitude, but his keeper must be sure to remove the remains if there be any the next day. The water should be changed often and kept sweet.

Turtles should be accommodated in a similar way, that is, with wet and dry places for choice. Two very " cute " little turtles lived happily once in the basin of a greenhouse fountain, with a rock-work mound on which to rest. They recognized persons, fed from the fingers, and grew very tame. What boys call the box-turtle, really a land-tortoise, will be, or at least appear, quite contented if he is " staked out " in the yard in this way: a hole carefully drilled in the edge of his shell, and a light cord a yard or two long tied through it, with the other end fastened to a stake. The animal proceeds at once to burrow a home for himself, and there he will dwell in seeming satisfaction, while his keeper can coax him out occasionally by pulling gently on the cord to look at him and see if he is doing well.

The Florida chameleon, which also is frequently brought home by the tourist, is a bright and intelligent creature. He requires almost unlimited sunshine to bask in, and flies, which he catches on the end of his long tongue, to eat. A fernery is a comfortable place for him. This fellow, it is said, has a temper, and if not well treated or if teased he shows fight, though he can hardly do much

17

harm. The genuine chameleon, after whom the Florida lizard is named, is one of the quaintest and oddest of pets; but he is a native of the Old World, and rarely seen in our country.

Another American of the family, often sent from the West and South to pet lovers, is called the horned toad, though he is no toad, but a lizard. He is said to be an interesting pet, and capable of being taught. All the small members of the reptile race live upon insects, and need to be kept in very warm quarters.

INDEX

THE END

W. HAMILTON GIBSON'S WORKS.

No one knows more of flowers, shrubs, trees, and birds than Mr. Gibson, or of the special haunts and homes of all of them : and even readers to whom botany is a sealed book may follow him into the fields and woods and marshes with a full certainty of being charmed and enlightened in unexpected ways.—*N. Y. Tribune.*

SHARP EYES: A Rambler's Calendar of Fifty-two Weeks among Insects, Birds, and Flowers. Illustrated by the Author. 8vo, Cloth, Ornamental, $5 00. (*In a Box.*)

STROLLS BY STARLIGHT AND SUN-SHINE. Illustrated by the Author. Royal 8vo, Cloth, Ornamental, $3 50.

HAPPY HUNTING-GROUNDS. Illustrated by the Author. 4to, Cloth, Ornamental, Gilt Edges, $7 50. (*In a Box.*)

HIGHWAYS AND BYWAYS. Illustrated by the Author. 4to, Cloth, Ornamental, Gilt Edges, $7 50. (*In a Box.*)

PASTORAL DAYS. Illustrated by the Author. 4to, Cloth, Ornamental, Gilt Edges, $7 50. (*In a Box.*)

CAMP LIFE IN THE WOODS, and the Tricks of Trapping and Trap Making. Illustrated by the Author. 16mo, Cloth, $1 00.